SONG TITLE SERIES

CLASSIC

50s & 60s

ROCK 'N' ROLL

JOAN MAGUIRE

Copyright Page

New: Classic 50s & 60s Rock 'N' Roll

Author: Joan Maguire

National Library of Australia Cataloguing-in-Publication – Publication entry

Creator:	Maguire, Joan, author
Title:	Classic 50s & 60s rock 'n' roll / Joan Maguire.
ISBN:	978-0-9941998-5-0 (paperback)
Series:	Song title series; 13
Notes:	Includes bibliography references
Subjects:	Short stories
	Titles of musical compositions--Fiction

Dewey Number: A823. 4

Published with the assistance of CreateSpace and is available on the Print on Demand Network and www.songtitleseries.com.

This soft cover short story book and cover was created and written By Joan Maguire on 19th July 2010 ©
ISBN: 978-0-9941998-5-0

E-book re-written July 2014©
EISBN: 978-0-9941998-4-3

This book was converted into large print in March 2015 © and is available through the same distributors as the normal book or www.songtitleseries.com
ISBN: 978-0-9943297-8-3 (large print)

DEDICATION

I would like to dedicate this book and say to thank you to my Earth Angel David and his friends, who inspire and motivate me to achieve things that I never dreamt, were possible.

INTRODUCTION

Legally I cannot use Lyrics or Music because of Copyright but I can use song titles (Italicized) so a total of 2062 song titles have been used to bring you this story. Also due to the nature of my books; legally I must place a Reference (exactly as it is down loaded) and Bibliography after the story.

I love Rock 'N' Roll, so I decided to use compilation albums from the 1950s and 1960s in this story that gave me a good selection of song titles and artists to use and choose from.

Jump in Molly's car and become a passenger as she sets out to find *Lucille* who has *runaway* again. Be with her when she meets some old friends along the way; like Bobby, who is walking *on the road again* trying to leave his past and a *secret love* he had in *Kansas City* behind. *Running Bear* and Yokomo who both tell her stories about some strange happenings from their surrounding area that could affect people: and *Long Tall Sally*. They all point her in the direction to where *Lucille* is heading.

Continue travelling with Molly and Bobby on their mystical journey until they reach *Memphis Tennessee* and meet up with *Lucille* at her Uncle Charlie's house where she tells Molly about things she has seen and heard on her trip, what she learned about the history and past happenings when *Memphis* and Mississippi were first founded, and how rock and roll first began, as told to her by a friend and her friend's mother.

Sit back, relax and start reading to find out what the strange happenings are and how they affect Molly, Bobby and *Lucille*. Don't forget that because of using the original song titles in whole, there are places in the book that could be changed to make it more comprehensible for you the reader

ACKNOWLEDGEMENTS

I would like to thank my daughters, Jenny and Kylie for their positive but critical input in the first draft of this book and all the help and support that they have given me throughout the Song Title Series books. With taking their input to mind, I have improved the book.

I would also like to thank my son Peter and his family for their support and help in keeping me grounded.

To my best friend Dawn, thank you for being there and supporting me. Somehow you always knew when I needed picking up with a good laugh.

I would like to thank Kay and Julie for their patience and understanding whilst teaching me and giving me the skills to present my unique books in the best way possible.

I would like to give a special mention to Google because they have so many good sites for me to research the information to use in my stories. Many times I gather information; however, the song titles dictate the story to me and I end up either not using the information or using just a snippet or two.

I would also like to thank everyone else who has helped me bring this book to life and to you for purchasing it.

OTHER BOOKS IN THE SONG TITLE SERIES

Bon Jovi – Wanted Dead Or Alive
Green Day
AC/DC
Beach Boys
Slim Dusty
Country Women
Five Country Men
Six Crooners
Three Crooners
ABBA
The Rat Pack
Elton John
Classic 50s & 60s Rock 'N' Roll

CONTENTS

Title Page
Copyright
Dedication
Introduction
Acknowledgements
Other Books In The Song Title Series
Chapter 1: Time To Move On   2
Chapter 2: The Girls   10
Chapter 3: Molly's Story   16
Chapter 4: A Magical Place   24
Chapter 5: Thinking Back   30
Chapter 6: Chasing Lucille   34
Chapter 7: A Great Day   39
Chapter 8: Lucille's Story   44
Chapter 9: A New Future   50
Chapter10: Meeting New Families   55
Chapter 11: Lucille's Party   61
Chapter 12: The Wedding Reception   66
Reference   72
Bibliography   121
About The Author   122
Testimonials   123

TIME TO MOVE ON

Not one vehicle had passed him since he had set out that day, so taking his time, *the wanderer* made his way along *Tobacco Road* towards the town of *Red River Rock*. So far it had been a long trek of *26 miles* from *Kansas City,* a big bustling crowded place; however, he was not in any hurry as the day was warm and sunny.

He enjoyed the peace and quiet of the countryside that was green and lush with the occasional sound of the *Mocking bird* coming from high in the trees that lined some parts of the road. He had tried for nearly three years to settle down and make a life for himself in one place but he had spent nearly all of his younger years *surfin' U.S.A.* and travelling overseas.

Africa was a different place than what he had expected it to be and whist he was there, *Fanny Mae* had taught him the *African Waltz*. She asked him one day "The *witch doctor* gave me something *so cone on a my house* and *baby let's play house*. I would really love to do the *chicken shack boogie* with you. *I just want to make love to you* for as long as I can."

He told her "*Baby, don't get hooked on me* as I have a *ticket to ride* and I am going to be using it the day after tomorrow. I am going to meet a friend, *Bony Maronie,* in a *Spanish Harlem* on the coast and I will be working on the *Shrimp boats* and *crawfishin'* until I have enough money to move on again. I want to go to Europe and spend *Christmas in Killarney*. I know it will be *Christmastime all over the world* but I am looking forward to a *white Christmas* for a change.

Last year, I spent Christmas in Australia and worked on an outback station as a *C.C.rider* mustering cattle on a *bad motorcycle* because the wind would blow the dust into the engine causing it to stop all the time.

The fat man, Tom Dooley said "*Come go with me* along *Tobacco Road* to the *Mony Mony* tribe's campsite in the *Jailhouse Rock* Valley. The *Mony Mony* is an indigenous tribe of people and today, their elder, *Jim Dandy* is going to tell another of his dreamtime stories."

As we approached we heard one of the kids yelling out "*Tie me kangaroo down;* I said *tie me kangaroo down mate*."

Tom said "I come here often and I will warn you; only drink *cool water* or you may end up spending the night with the *devil woman* of the tribe. *They call her La Bamba* but her real name is Cathy and all she wants to do is *hit, git and split* with all your cash and leaving you feeling like *Cathy's clown* and a fool. I was *Cathy's clown* once and she had me so drunk that all I can remember was saying "tell that *bird dog* to *drink up thy zider.*" and waking up with a really bad *fever.*"

I still remember when *Jim Dandy* came out and sat in the shade of several tall gum trees. The first thing he said was "*Johnny b goode* and give our guests a cool drink and some of our type of *ginger bread.*"

The wanderer continued "He then looked me in the eyes, something they don't normally do, and continued speaking "*Time after time* and after many a *blue moon* has passed through the night sky, the *twilight time* brings us the *silhouettes* of *yesterday* and yesteryears. These silhouettes are the spirits of the earth; you would call them Earth Angels, who help people who are lost in many different ways.

Beyond the sea are many more adventures for you but you will still get the *summertime blues* and no sort of healing, including *sexual healing,* will stop them. You will never be a true *gamblin' man* but you will take chances that will not work like you planned. At some stage of your life you will once again stay in a *Heartbreak Hotel* but the *heartaches by the number* will only be few. *Don't be cruel* to the ones who make you feel *downhearted* because *you're the one* who controls your emotions.

You may try to be *the great pretender* but *the heart of a man* in *a world without love* is just a *cold cold heart.* At the moment *you've lost that loving feeling,* but *the green leaves of summer,* a night of *a thousand stars,* a *blue moon* and a *brown eyed girl* with *broken wings* will make you feel like you have gone *from a Jack to a king.* Be a *daydream believer* and *keep a knockin'* on *the green door.*

One day *when you walk in the room* your *dream lover* will be there and you will find that you *can't help falling in love* with her. She will not be a *calendar girl* but she will be *the living doll* and the *little bitty pretty one* that you search for. *Try to remember* that *under the moon of love,* the *two hearts of stone* will be *walkin' back to happiness* together. It *all depends on you* and *only you* to say *hello little girl* to start you both down the path of *true love ways.*

A windmill in old Amsterdam will not bring the *good vibrations* even though it will be *an affair to remember. Believe what you say* and *you'll never walk alone* again as an *Earth Angel* will always be with you even if you can't see them and you can speak to them any time and they will hear you."

3

He looked at Tom and said "*I got my mojo working* because *up above my head I hear music in the air* and he will also hear it in time. The *unchained melody* of love will be his signal to *let the good times roll* again."

He left Australia and continued his travelling for another year and then returned home and once *back in the U.S.A.* went *surfin' U.S.A.*, before meeting up with *Iki Iko* in *Surf City* who had arranged some work for him in the *evenin' time* at *the Hokey Pokey* Fun Arcade in *Galveston*.

Unbeknown to him, the *F.B.I.* had an undercover agent working at the Arcade as they had a *suspicion* that some new drug called *Chi Chi* was being sold through the premises and *the finger of suspicion* was pointed at *Hoots Mon* and his girlfriend, *Susie Q* who was also known as *Cherry Pie.*

Chi Chi was known to be that dangerous that it could put people in an *endless sleep;* but what the base ingredient of *Chi Chi* was, was still to be discovered.

Hoots Man, who had been down on his luck for many years had recently been able to afford a *brand new Cadillac* for himself and had bought his girlfriend several new outfits that were made from some very expensive *Chantilly lace.*

The first night he arrived at the Arcade, the *F.B.I.* questioned him for a few hours and then said "*Hit the road Jack* or *the chances* are that you might get the *Folsom Prison Blues* if you end up getting involved with the rest of the staff here."

He jumped a *freight train in the still of the nite* and ended up in Kansas City. Since arriving in Kansas City, he had been working as a *handy man* for *Mr Lee* who ran a *Honky Tonk* bar in *New Orleans,* a suburb of Kansas City, but the *summertime blues* and the *Western movies* being shown around town made him feel like it was time to move on; time to get *on the road again.*

The day before he left, *Speedy Gonzalas,* the owner of *Hernando's Hideaway* Restaurant, came rushing into the bar of the café where he was having a coffee all excited saying "*Ding Dong The Witch Is Dead;* that Witch Hazel plant that has been growing by my front door is finally gone.

Come on *let's go, let's go, let's go, let's have a party* down in *Palisades Park* before you go. We will *rock around the clock, jump, jive an' wail* and we will eat lots of food because *Mack the knife* will be

4

cooking steak, *green onions, mashed potatoes* and his special sauce made from *Cherry Stones* over *great balls of fire* like he always does. I will supply lots of *Tequila* and Apricot *Sherry* and Mr *Do Wah Diddy Diddy* from *The House Of The Rising Sun* will provide *Sukiyaki* wine.

Dede Dinah Medley said that she will supply the *Peppermint Twist, Nut Rocker,* The King Bee, *Blueberry Hill* and *Sugarbush* flavored ice cream for deserts. *I'm a King Bee lover,* but personally I like a scoop of that and *Peppermint Twist* together. *Poke Salad Annie* said that she will supply some of her famous salads, and some of her homemade *shortnin' bread.*

Please say you will come for a while and *then you can tell me goodbye.* My *mama says* that *on the street where you live,* your *friends and neighbours* are saying *ain't it shame* that you have decided to leave and I know that you will be missed by many more people around here."

When he got to the party, there was a *whole lot of shakin'* going on; people doing the *Brotosaurus Stomp* and the *Hippy Hippy Shake.* Even *Her Royal Majesty* and the *Duke Of Earl* attended and they had arrived *in a golden coach.* While they were walking past the *Entry of the Gladiators,* a jumping castle for the children, the Earl's messenger interrupted them and said "*Milord,* a message has just been received by *Royal Telephone* that Sir *William Tell Overture* would like you to *Tell Laura I Love Her* and that the wife of *the purple people eater* will be *the stripper* this evening and she will be wearing her *itsy bitsy teeny weeny yellow polka dot bikini.*"

The Earl turned around to the *purple people eater* who was walking behind both of them humming *Ob La Di Ob La Da* and said "Did you know that your wife was performing here tonight?" and the purple people eater replied "Oh yes and she will be wearing her *itsy bitsy teeny weeny yellow polka dot bikini.* When her act is finished, we will go on to the party and she will *save the last dance for me* like she always does."

Her Majesty looked at the Earl and said "Although I think *you've got personality,* I also think *you talk too much.* Now *let's walk that-a-way* and have some *fun, fun, fun* watching the *Sheik of Araby shake rattle and roll* whilst he is dancing the *rock-a-billy boogie* with *short Fat Fannie.* The *Rocking Pneumonia and Woogie Blues* band is one of the best bands around and it's a pity that I had to *hang up my rock and roll shoes* when I became Queen."

There were *girls, girls, girls* everywhere; however, the Earl stopped one girl and said "*Little darlin',* I remember you. Aren't you a calendar girl from the Kon Tiki Rocket 88 Men's Club?

Isn't your name something like *Diane, Diana* or is it *Eloise?"*

The girl replied "No sir, I am *Elenore,* a *Tallahassee lassie* on a *summer holiday* here. Our band, *I'm the Urban Spaceman* will be singing tonight. *Cliff Richard Medley,* his brother *Elvis Medley, Linda Lu* and I will be on the *Lily of Laguna* stage just after eight o'clock."

Good golly Miss Molly was also there dressed to *razzle dazzle the In Crowd* in her bright red sequin top and her black skirt with contrasting red sequin *hound dog* motives sewn down one side of the skirt. Her hair was pinned back with a comb that had black and red ribbons flowing from it but normally *she wears red feathers* in her hair.

In another section of the park there were *little children* flying *kites* or playing with a *rubber ball.* There were people standing around an Australian who turned and said to another man "You had better *tie me kangaroo down sport* as he will want to go and play with the kids and he can be a bit of a *wild thing.* Don't worry; I won't throw this thing in my hand because *my boomerang won't come back* anyway; even if I did throw it."

Someone said "Did you know that he's *the man who shot Liberty Valance* in the paint ball skirmish?"

A reply came as the group of people walked away "Yes, I heard that finally someone has beaten Liberty but no-one knew who he was. Are you sure that he's *the man who shot Liberty Valance* and ended his winning streak?"

Runaround Sue was telling her friend and some other people about the *Ode to Billy Joe,* when someone yelled out "Hey look there's *three coins in a fountain* over here and a *little ship. I remember the Cornfields* and *Itchycoo Park* where a *Kentucky woman* named *Nellie Dean* would play *rock and roll music* on *Saturday nite at the duck pond* there. She also had a fountain for people to donate *money* for a charity in the district. The organization that she collected money for helped the *young ones* from her district *get a job."*

The party grew so big and noisy that there were even people *dancing in the street.* He even just heard someone yell out *"Hey Paula,* love your *Chantilly lace* dress. *Honey don't* rush to *shake baby shake* because down *at the hop,* at the moment, *The Old Piano Roll Blues* band is playing *The Petite Waltz, the Homing Waltz at the end of the day* and *the theme from the Threepenny Opera* for the *Lovey Dovey* dance exhibition; but soon they will start playing the *Hippy Hippy Shake* music again."

He stayed for a few hours; had *one mint Julep, a shot of rhythm and blues* with *La Bamba* Sykes who was a *hound dog man* and trainer, his *little bitty pretty one, little miss Ruby* and his son *Raunchy;* then left the party and went back to his small apartment and packed his few belongings in his knapsack. He thought that late afternoon or early *night time is the right time* to leave because just about everyone was down at the party and there wouldn't be so much of a fuss made.

He had already told the apartment manager that he was leaving and as he handed back his key, the manager said *"Danke schoen* and take care. If you are ever back this way again, call in and spend some time as *there's always room at our house* for a visitor. If you ever move back here though, I will always find you a place 'cos you were one of my good tenants; not like some who use this place as *the battle of New Orleans* battle field."

The first evening on the road he walked under a *blue moon* until he reached the *McDonald's Cave* Diner, which was really just a truck stop and layover place. He went inside and noticed that there were a few truck drivers sitting at a couple of tables, talking and drinking coffee from very large mugs. He also saw a few more people, who he thought, may have been travelers and had just stopped for a break and a quick meal.

A couple who were just leaving said to one another *"We've gotta get out of this place* and *on the road again. What a difference a day makes* when you're only *twenty four hours from Tulsa* and home."

He also noticed a sign on the wall that read "OVERNIGHT BUNKS $5.00".

He sat at a table situated against the wall, not far from the door and looked at the menu. A few minutes later the waitress came over and took his order and as she walked back to the kitchen, one of the truck drivers called out *"Susie darlin',* could you please bring me two scoops of *Tutti Frutti* ice-cream and some change for the jukebox."

She kept walking and said to the man "Only two scoops this time? Be there in a minute."

He went over to the jukebox and noticed that most of the songs were ones that the kids would play down *at The Hop.* "So *rock and roll is here to stay."* he said quietly to himself and he selected a couple of songs before he returned to his table as the waitress brought his meal over.

While he was eating his meal, *the wanderer* heard the truck drivers

7

talking about the *forty miles of bad road* that lay ahead and the man with the *red Cadillac and a black moustache.*

"He was a maniac driving and drinking from a *bottle of wine.* He was certainly *a must to avoid* because *you never can tell* where those sorts of drivers are going to end up. *I can't help myself* from wanting to run them off the road just to teach them a lesson. He came flying passed me like he was in a *race with the Devil* and nearly ran the *little deuce coupe* in front of me off the road. *I got a woman* friend in *Galveston* who is now singing the *ballad of a teenage queen* because a drunk driver put her *little bitty pretty one* in a wheel chair for the rest of her life." said one driver.

"I know what you mean." said another driver "*I go ape* when some stupid driver thinks that they are the only *one outside of heaven.* We all see it *over and over* again. With speeding and other distractions that they are doing, they are really heading for the *last farewell.* Before they know it; *Sh-boom* and they are going *up up and away* in an *endless sleep* from the people who love them. We all know that not *only love can break a heart* but also the loss of someone dear to us. If they don't die they can end up disabled and living in a *poor me* world that is also not very good for the rest of their families who have to look after them because of their stupidity."

Another driver put down his coffee cup and added "I agree with you about some drivers who think that they're in a *race with the Devil.* *Sixteen tons* is hard to stop suddenly; it takes a minute of two just to *slow down* so you can get *all shook up* when you do see someone driving erratically.

Just outside *Perfidia,* the Highway Patrol Officers have a field day with speeders. I see them there quite often and that's why I have a warning bell attached to my *speedoo* to tell me when I am over the speed limit. My license is my livelihood, and it is so important to me that I don't do anything stupid that would make the Highway Patrol Officers want to put me in the judicial system where they could take my license and *rip it up,* leaving me without a source of income that I love doing. I think that those drivers who *rave on* about what they do and how they have never been caught doing it, are in for a shock on *one fine day* in the near future."

He was interrupted as one of the other drivers said "Thank you *Susie darlin'.*" as she put his apple pie with cream and ice cream down in front of him.

Then he continued "*Peter Gunn* was an old friend and he used to take *Robin Hood*ney to the club and everytime Peter wanted to leave,

Robin used to say "What's your rush. Let's have *another little drink* before we go."

One morning his misses was at *my front door* all hysterical and told me that Peter and Robin had been in an accident. You see, *there was a tall Oak tree* just across from the entrance of the club's car park and when they left Peter was behind the wheel then Robin decided that he wanted to drive and grabbed the wheel causing the car to swerve straight into the tree. Thankfully both men were not seriously hurt but the cars a right off and it put a big damper on the friendship and Peter won't drive Robin anywhere anymore."

As *Susie Q* gave the truck driver his ice cream she said "Did you hear about the man on *the Isle of Innisfree* who sat *up on the roof* of the local hotel with a *shotgun* and he would *fire* at anybody who came out of the hotel drunk and go to get into their vehicle to drive home. He never hit anyone but it was enough to frighten them so they wouldn't try to get in and drive.

The police tried to coax him down from the roof but he stayed put and yelled at them to "*Dust my broom* and give it to the next drunk who comes out the door. Two days later at *twilight time* he left the roof and was arrested. I haven't heard anything more."

Listening to their *yakety yak* about other drivers made him decided to *stay* the night there and start out early the next day. "It would be safer because *I'm walkin'* and I may not be seen *in the still of the night* by other motorists." he thought.

The waitress showed him where the bunks and washrooms were, then handed him a towel as he paid her and said good night. The waitress said that she needed a name for the books and he said his name was Bobby.

THE GIRLS

Bobby woke early the next day feeling relaxed. The bunk had been surprisingly comfortable and he had slept well. He went into the diner for some breakfast before heading off. The truck drivers were already gone and were most probably many miles down the road on the way to their destinations and he noticed that there was a different waitress on that morning.

She wore a *lavender blue* uniform with *blue suede shoes* and she seemed to be only five feet tall. She also had blue eyes and long blonde hair tied back into a ponytail. He thought that if she were the *devil with the blue dress on,* then she was the *little bitty pretty one.*

Bobby sat at the same table as he had the previous evening but was startled when the waitress spoke and asked him for his order. He thought that she had *come softly to me.* A short time later he had finished his meal and had started walking down the road.

A few miles down the road he felt a few *raindrops* but it didn't amount to much. He looked up at the clouds but they had all nearly passed over. He thought to himself "*I don't know why but I do* love *just walkin' in the rain* and when the *raindrops keep fallin' on my head* it makes me feel so alive and not to mention wet."

He walked a great distance that day without seeing anyone, except for a couple of cars traveling in the opposite direction, while the sun hid behind the clouds for most of the time. Then he approached a sign that read "*SCORPIO* 10 MILES AHEAD. Population 3,500"

"If I can make it there today, then I'll stay the night. I might be able to hitch a ride to *somewhere* ahead tomorrow." he thought. "Those truck drivers weren't wrong about this road really being bad as it's making me quite tired. I can also see *why* there hasn't been much traffic on this stretch of road. The motorists must be taking a detour past the *Grand Coulee Dam* to *Apache* and then on to *Surf City.*"

After walking for what seemed to be hours, he finally reached the town. He saw some children playing with a *rubber ball* and asked "*Hey little girl* could you please tell me if there is a hotel or motel anywhere near?"

The girl pointed down the road and said "Way *down yonder,* there is mister."

He thanked her and kept walking until he reached the motel and booked a room for the night. He thought "*If I didn't have a dime,* I would have to try and work for food and a bed like I did when I stayed over to feel *Nairobi swingin'* with *Reet Petite.* Those *Spanish eyes* of hers made many a head turn when she walked into the *Harlem Nocturne* Café."

After resting awhile at the motel, he ventured out to find a place to eat and not far from the motel he found a diner. He went in and sat down in a booth that was next to a group of young women who seemed to be trying to console one of the girls who was *crying.*

He could not help but overhear the girls saying "*Oh Carol,* I told you that *he will break your heart.* The girls he takes out and then dumps always end up in *tears.*"

Someone else said "*My heart cries for you* and he may be a *brown-eyed handsome man* with a *baby face,* but *I'm telling you now* that he's just a no good *sweet talkin' guy.* It's one of the *games people play* and if you play long enough you can get *dizzy* from it. You should ask *Mustang Sally* what he's like. When she was *living next door to Alice,* she went over to pick up the pieces of the *broken doll* that he left behind when he dumped Alice."

Then he heard "*Oh Carol,* he likes playing *the crying game* with the girls he knows. I know that you were *so much in love* with him but he's just a *rebel rouser. He'll have to go* 'cos you're too good for him. If he can't *respect* the girls he goes out with, then they won't want to know him."

"Say *bye, bye Johnny* and forget him. I know *it keeps right on a hurtin'* for a while but you'll be like a *rubber ball* and you'll bounce back quickly. Johnny is just like the guy in the movie "*Rise & fall of Flingal Bunt.*" He made *promises, promises* to all the girls he met and soon they got wise to him. He was soon saying *there goes my baby; somebody stole me gal* from me and after *seven drunken nights* he was *singing the blues to all the girls I have loved before.*"

"Yes, say *danke schoen* and *auf wiederseh'n sweetheart* to the *bad boy* especially if he gets his friends to say "*Tell Laura I love her.*" He often gets his so called mates to pass on messages for him, and usually it is "Tell whoever his last girl was that I love her" but they are now not passing the messages on and are avoiding him. He will soon know how *only the lonely* feel and he won't like it."

The waitress came over and Bobby asked what the Diner's Special was and she said "*Dixie fried* chicken burger with fries and a drink."

He placed his order and as he did, one of the girls from the booth next him went to the jukebox and put on the songs *Rock Around the Clock* and *Reveille Rock*. "*Hello Mary Lou*." said the girl at the jukebox as another female passed her.

Mary Lou went to the booth with the other girls then said "*Oh Carol, everybody's somebody's fool* and *I heard it through the grapevine* from Stag, who is mighty happy now, about what has just happened. I think that you should know that Johnny's mother brought him here from *Galveston* a few years ago because his father ran off with another woman and her *mother-in-law* was so *la dee dah* that she made his mother feel like she didn't belong anymore.

Since then Johnny's mother has told him that as he *became muncho,* he thought that he was a *big man* but he isn't, he's just *a little boy lost.* She also said to him that you have not gone from a *jack to a king,* but you're a *real wild child* now; *you're no good* and *your cheatin'* heart will only bring you down. Look what happened to the *big green car* when you took *Claudette* out. You had to sell it to get the *money honey* because *on top of old Smokey* you got her pregnant and now she has *twenty tiny fingers* to love and bring up. Don't tell me that you were *not responsible* because you know you were, and it will be the *twelfth of never* before you admit it.

You should see him at home now because when his mother is around, *Sh-boom* he becomes a *robot man* and won't even say *Tweedlee dee* to her. Don't forget that I have lived next door to him since they moved in and that's just a part of what his mother shouted to him during their *last fight* last week."

Then she added "*I remember you* telling me not so long ago that *you're sixteen* and you were *born free* and want to live your life to the beat of a *different drum.* Well, do so; *you got what it takes* so when you see him, just walk on by humming *Ob-la-di, Ob-la-da* and don't let him see what he's done by upsetting you. Let him see that his *words* and actions don't have any effect on you and if he stops you and wants to talk; just tell him that *you don't own me* and I'm *walking back to happiness* and to someone else but don't tell him who."

Carol replied "I know that *he'll have to go* and I'll get over him *with a little help from my friends* but it's hard to say *bye bye love* so quickly. I didn't know that *Stagger Lee* even knew that I was alive; now he could be *my boy lollipop* as he is so sweet."

He had just about finished his meal when the music stopped and one of the girls said *"C'mon everybody,* back to my place, *Hawaii Five-O* will be on soon. I love watching Danno.

You know that *Stagger Lee* will be very, very happy now that you are free again. *Stagger Lee, he's so fine* and those *blue suede shoes* that he wears. I would give anything to have those *lovin' arms* wrapped around me. I would love to say to him *hold me, thrill me, kiss me* and *more, more, more* but he's not *my guy* and he's not *lookin' for love* from me."

Then the girls left and he followed them out the door and stood on the sidewalk wondering if he wanted to go back to the motel straight away. As the girls disappeared from sight, the thought of being *a teenager in love* and *a teenage romance* entered his mind. *Only love can break a heart* but *why do fools fall in love* all the time and continuously get hurt?

You would think that being *only sixteen* was *too young* to understand what *the power of love* is really like. I don't think that I even know myself but I do know that the tears from the hurt that you feel, is like when *smoke gets in your eyes* and irritates them for days.

He decided to have a quick look around the town and then head back to the motel. Bobby made his way back past the *Chapel of Love,* that he had made as a landmark for himself, to the motel and although it was still early, he was now so tired from all the walking that he had done that day that he went to bed and fell asleep straight away.

During the night an *Earth Angel* came to him in a dream and said *"You always hurt the one you love.* Why did you *runaway?* What are you *searchin' for?* I know that *you've got your troubles* and that *you've lost that lovin' feeling* but *only you and you alone* can do something about it. Will you become *the great pretender* and try to forget that *Cupid* shot you with his *little arrows,* because if you do then *you'll lose a good thing?* No amount of *wishin' and hopin'* could stop you from *singing the blues,* so *baby come back* to the real world; because *you are my destiny* to help and in a way *you belong to me* and to someone else who will love you in the very near future."

Bobby woke with a start, jumped out of bed and looked around. He was *shaking all over.* *"She's not there,* I must have been dreaming but it seemed so real. I must be *going out of my head* and I never knew that *my heart is an open book* for she knew how I was feeling inside."

He looked around again to remind himself that there's *nobody be me* in this room. He was so wound up by his so-real dream that he found it hard to go back to bed, so he turned on the TV and started to watch an old

13

movie called *Hats off to Larry* that was about *heroes and villains.*

"Someone's coming." said one of the villains as he grabbed the biggest money bags from the safe.

One of the heroes said to the villains "*Get down, get down on the floor* or I'll put you in an *endless sleep.* I know that behind those masks you are the *Beatnik Fly* and *Be-Bop-A-Lula.*"

"Well, *hat's off to Larry* for finding us; but how did he do it?" said *Be-Bop-A-Lula* as she turned to run away. Shots were fired then she said "*Bang bang he shot me down. I don't know why I do* but I feel *dizzy* and I only caught the bullet in my arm."

Larry walked through the door and said "Ah, *it must be him,* the *leader of the pack.* Looking for you might have been like looking for a *needle in a haystack* but you were overheard talking in *Perfidia* about this heist. Now it looks like that you're both going *down the line* but *Beatnik Fly* you're going down the *Rock Island line* for a long time. *Be-Bop-A-Lula,* I think the *Allentown Jail* for women is where you will end up living for quite a while."

Be-Bop-A-Lula said "Beatnik I always said *you talk too much.* Your mouth is always in a *race with the Devil* and you win every time."

Beatnik replied "*Ya ya, ya ya, yeh yeh, yakety yak, yakety yak* always telling me off, that's all you do. I think that going to jail just to get away from you would be one of the good things that could happen to me."

He changed the channel as that movie didn't interest him and started watching *Great Balls Of Fire* another old movie about *A Scottish Soldier.* When he turned the channel over, the movie was already part the way through to where two people were shouting at each other while *the Moulin Rouge theme* played in the background.

The first person said "*What kind of fool do you think I am.* I know that *we won't live in a castle* but *you cash ain't nothing but trash* and I know about *the poor people of Paris* and how it's a gun*fire- crazy world. Don't treat me like a child* or you'll be *walking to New Orleans* after I've kicked you out."

The second person replied "*You don't have to say you love me* but won't you *come go with me* to *Bongo Rock.* We could hitch a ride on the *six-five special fast freight train.* It pulls up near *Jailhouse Rock* to load more fuel before carrying on to *Dragnet* Hollow where my sister lives.

If you don't want to go to either place, then we can catch the *Cincinnati Fireball* Express and get right away from *Bony Maronie.*"

The first person then said "Don't you understand; *Bony Maronie, he's out of my life* and I *ain't misbehavin'* with you either."

He wasn't interested in that movie either so he turned off the TV and went back to bed. It took him awhile to get back to sleep and when he did, he slept well without any more dreams or interruptions.

After he woke and dressed early the following morning, he set off for the diner for some breakfast and to find out if there was someone around that he could hitch a ride out of town with.

When he entered the diner he was surprised to see a woman he knew sitting near the counter and he approached her and said "*Good golly Miss Molly* what are you doing here?"

MOLLY'S STORY

Molly was startled by the sudden mention of her name. She had been *a thousand miles away* thinking about her past and what had led her to be where she was at that moment.

She recalled how she would *rock around the clock* with her girlfriend *rockin' Robin* and how they would often go to the *Red River Rock* dance classes where their teachers, *Rebel Rouser* and *Reet Petite* would teach them *reelin' and rockin'* moves. On one occasion, *Rebel Rouser* came to teach the classes with what he called the *rocking pneumonia & the boogie woogie flu.*

Then as the years rolled on, *rockin' Robin* moved to Tennessee and learned the *Tennessee waltz* and *rock-a-billy,* which is danced to faster *rock & roll* music. She wrote and said that she had a new dance partner, *Billy Riley,* who she described as *poetry in motion,* and I love him in his *blue suede shoes*. I am still *a teenager in love* with rock and roll and I hope that in time Billy and I could do *the wedding samba* together. *I heard it through the grapevine* that *rockin' Robin* became a *calendar girl* in the *Rock Island Line Rock On* magazine and moved to California to become one of the *California girls* leaving her partner to dance with *Diana* or *Corinna, Corinna* or somebody new.

She remembered that through her parents, she met a *travelin' man* who told her of some of his expeditions. She particularly liked the ones where he was *stranded in the jungle* with his guide who told him that *the lion sleeps tonight* but the *tiger* is still on the prowl and will be until the *click clack* noises from other animals cease.

The other story was when he was *the lonely surfer* and a *stranger in Paradise,* who was *sittin' on the dock of the bay,* when he heard that there was a *whole lotta shakin' goin' on* down on the river bank. A *whole lotta woman* approached him and said that *Cara Mia* was from the *land of 1000 dances* and she would *teach you to rock* to the music of *Rock 'N' Roll Deacon Screamin* band, *the Adoration Waltz* to *the song from Moulin Rouge* or *the Locomotion* to some other type of *Rock and Roll* music.

It was a few months later that I sent *a message to Martha,* my cousin who lived in Miami and told her that I was coming for a *vacation.*

During the visit, the girls were at the beach nearly every day enjoying the *heatwave* that was unusual for that time of year and they saw

16

Johnny B. Goode and his friend who was a *brown eyed handsome man* walking towards them.

Martha said "Oh look; Here comes my *Johnny angel* and I wish that he was my *little darlin'*. He moved here from *Apache* four years ago with his parents and I see him just about every day. He caught me writing *love letters in the sand* one day and I also had *lonely teardrops* on my cheeks. He stopped and we started talking and he told me that *everybody needs someone to love* and that as I was *only sixteen* I would be silly *pledging my love* to one person now, as I had a lot of living to do first.

I thought about what he said and it seemed to make sense, but that hasn't stopped me from writing *love letters in the sand*. I also asked myself "*What do you want* to do in the future?"

A month later we were at the *Rock Island Line* Car Show and *Rock-A-Billy* Carnival weekend and there was a *brand new Cadillac* that had been modified and a *Stingray* that had been lowered and made into a convertible. Both cars looked like that they could win a *race with the devil.*

Anyway, when the band started playing *the French Can-Can Polka, Johnny B. Goode* walked up to me and asked "*Do you want to dance?*" and *oh what a nite* I had because there were *pretty girls everywhere* and he chose to spend the evening with me.

The carnival is over now but I still remember seeing him walking towards me like *poetry in motion* wearing *a white sport coat,* blue jeans and *blue suede shoes.*

Then *along came Jones* and *zing went the strings of my heart* and I immediately thought that I *got to get you into my life*. He joined *John* and as they walked over to us John called out to another female who was sun baking "*Wake up little Susie* or you'll be burnt on one side and you won't be able to do a *whole lot of shakin tonight* 'cos there'll be a *whole lotta shakin' going on at the Hop* over at *the Mule Skinner Blues* Hall."

Jones stayed with us for the rest of the day and he even walked to the *bus stop* with us and we agreed to meet him that night *at the Hop*. He was my *brown eyed handsome man* who was also a *theme for a dream* and maybe one of the *three steps to Heaven* and the *Chapel of Love*. I know that I am only *seventeen* and a *sweet little rock and roller* but he is the one who could take me from *bobby sox to stockings*. I thought "*If I put a spell on you* to *love me tender* forever; how would I do it?"

I spent the rest of my vacation with Martha and Jones and when it was time for me to go home, Jones surprised me at the *bus stop* when he informed me that he would be coming back to Kansas City with me as he has some part time work there.

On the bus he told me "I *ain't got no home* of my own to go to and I have become *the wanderer* looking for a place to settle down. I come *from Russia with love*. I lived in a village called *Domino* with all the *dear hearts and gentle people* and a place where you are taught to *be true to your school motto* no matter how old you are.

I left home for many reasons but the main one was because *the girl of my best friend, Day-O* wanted to mess around with me behind *Day-O's* back. When I said to her "*What kind of fool am I* to even think about messing around with you? I *ain't misbehavin'* and *he will break your heart* when I tell him what you are up to. I know that you *ain't too proud to beg* but all your *diamonds and pearls* won't stop Day-O from saying *see you later alligator*. *Everybody's somebody's fool* but I won't be yours so *have yourself a merry little Christmas* and *let it snow, let it snow, let it snow* because I won't be here; I'll be in a warmer climate somewhere in this world."

I have travelled a lot and I have always found some sort of work that enabled me to pay my way. In one job at a Carnival, *I'm the Urban Spaceman* who played *Shake, Rattle and Roll* on the *Morningtown Ride*. The *Raunchy* Steam Engine was great to work on except when the wind was blowing in the wrong direction because that's when the *smoke gets in your eyes* making them water. Another time, *me and Mrs Jones* went to investigate a report that there were hazardous obstacles placed in the Jungle Maze and we got *stranded in the jungle* and had to get another carnie to get us out. I worked in the *Splish Splash* Ice-cream Parlor selling *Tutti Frutti* and *Spooky* Cones. *Spooky* Cones were a *medley* of different fruits mixed with *Tutti Frutti* or a different flavored ice-cream.

I used to like watching *Mr Sandman* with the children at the *Ivory Tower*. He would say "*Ready Teddy* or *Diana;* now *stand by me* and just throw the *rubber ball* at the *Mule Train* and knock *Tweedlee Dee* or the *bird dog* down." *The train kept a rollin around and around* and once the child knocked *Tweedlee Dee* or the *bird dog* down a *bip bop bip* sound was heard and he would say "*Oh Boy* or *oh little girl,* you have won a prize."

"*I've got a lovely bunch of coconuts* here for you to knock off the sticks. *Hey little girl;* Hey Mister, just one dollar will give you five chances to win a prize." *Volare* would shout from the stall opposite the *Ivory Tower*.

My last job was at the *Ferry Boat Inn* as a crowd controller when they would *rock around the clock* and as a crew member on the *Ferry across the Mersey*.

I have been just about *everywhere* on *trains & boats & planes* and I have *no regrets* with my life so far; except for having to peel *green onions* by hand every day for three months at a restaurant in *Spanish Harlem* but I would like to work more on boats and ships.

I have wondered many times *"What am I living for?"* and now I know. *Have I told you lately that I love you* and *I only have eyes for you?* I would like to start writing my *book of love* with you, starting from today? *When a man loves a woman,* he'll do all he can to make her happy and contented and he decided to get work as a seaman because the pay was very good and it would not take him long to earn enough money to be able to get a real home for himself and his new family that he wanted to start.

Molly said "I am looking for a *runaway* named *Lucille*. She is wearing a *lavender blue* dress and *blue suede shoes* and she has a white *Raunchy* bag. I think that she may be with another *young girl*. Both girls act like *sweet little sixteen* year olds but you can't tell if this other girl is a *devil or angel*. Have you seen a young girl fitting her description while on your travels?"

He told her that the only female that was dressed in a similar way to the girl she was looking for, was the waitress who was a lot older, back at the truck stop. While they sat and ate ham and eggs for breakfast, they talked a bit. Molly said that she was heading up the road further to *Red River '81* miles away and would give him a lift if he wanted to join her. He gratefully accepted, went back to the motel, gathered his belongings and then they drove away together.

Driving away from Scorpio, Bobby noticed how the countryside was still lush and green although there were some hills in the distance that were rapidly approaching. Miss Molly tuned the car's radio into the local station and a song came over the radio that was different from what he had been used to hearing.

He turned to Miss Molly and said *"Ain't that a shame,* we missed hearing the title to that song because I liked it."

19

Miss Molly said "That song's called *a Lover's Concerto* and I have heard it a few times before. Yes, it is a beautiful song although *rock and roll is here to stay*. Tell me do you know *what becomes of the broken hearted?"*

He stated that he didn't know and asked *"Why?"*

Then she said "Bobby, I have known you for the past two years, ever since you were in *Kansas City*. You always looked like you were living on *lonely street* and you were always searching *endlessly* for something or was it someone.

I was a bit like you many years ago, then *along came Jones*. After I had just finished senior *high school* and it was a *swingin' school*. I went to Miami for a vacation with my cousin who lived there and that's where I met Jones. One day, after we had been going together for a while he said *"Do you wanna make love?"* We had been *at The Hop* and the *rock and roll music* made me think that it was *a rockin' good way to mess around and fall in love*. We had a *groovy kind of love* happening for a while; then I fell pregnant and he went and got a permanent job as a sailor on the ship *THE HUCKLEBUCK*.

On his last trip home we spent his last day shopping for the baby and as we were walking back to the hotel that we were spending the night in*, a nightingale sang in Berkeley Square* and Jones said "Please, *come go with me* to see one of the *western movies* playing in town or to the Arcade and listen to *Tweedlee Dee singing the blues* as I try to get a little boat to *sail along silv'ry moon paths* to the prize ring. He won a big stuffed sleeping lion."

He promised to *stand by me* but then when he was back at sea, a storm broke and some *lightnin' strikes* hit the ship and it began sinking. The ship and all the crew were lost before another ship; the *DA DOO RON RON* reached the scene.

I recall that after *the cruel sea* took Jones from me, I was *sitting on the dock of the bay* and I saw the *DA DOO RON RON* sailing back into port and it was then that I started thinking of saying *goodbye cruel world* myself and how would I do it and where. When I was personally informed of what had happened, *all I could do was cry,* I was *all shook up* and I was *too weak to fight* all the emotions I was going through so I laid down on a *crimson and clover* colored blanket, said *goodbye cruel world* and took some pills hoping *the end of the world* would come soon. *Willie and the Hand Jive* crew found me and they did their best to help me make it through the night.

It was after *Willie and the Hand Jive* crew saved me and as Lucille was being born that I said to myself "Jones, *I'll always be in love with you* and *because of you* I have a daughter now and she is my future so I have to stop *living in the past*. I know that it is *easier said than done* and I will have *problems* but *whatever will be will be*.

You were the first of *my three steps to Heaven* and she is the second step. God only know who or what the third step is and I'll have to wait to find out. I will *cherish* your memory and *when my little girl is smiling* then I will always thank you for it.

Three months later, just after giving birth to my daughter, I was rocking her in the *cradle of love* that Jones had bought her on one of his home visits, when I received *the letter* that Jones had written and posted the day before the storm. There was a lot of *yakety yak* nonsense in it but he always started his letters with "this letter is *dedicated to the one I love*." and he also wrote *how sweet it is to be loved by you* and I keep wondering *will you love me tomorrow* because I'll still love you. He would finish his letter by writing "this is from your *sailor boy,* sailing on a *sea of love* back to you and this letter is *sealed with a kiss*." Jones and then he would write in capital letters *P. S.I LOVE YOU* followed by some hand drawn hearts.

He would always *come softly to me* in my dreams and I would always say to myself *please Mr Postman* bring me a letter to say that he is safe and well and is coming back to us.

My daughter's name is *Lucille* and she is the *runaway* that I'm looking for. She was hanging around with *Runaround Sue* and a friend of hers who suggested *let's have a party.*

They came and asked me if they could have one at my house and I said "No". *Because they're young,* they live their lives to the beat of a *different drum* to me and treated me like *poison ivy* and she doesn't understand why I don't allow her to do some things or go to some places. If she had to *walk a mile in my shoes,* then she would understand that even with a small fire, *smoke gets in your eyes* and can blind you from all who really matter to you."

Then she went quiet and he asked "*How do you do it,* and how did you keep the existence of your daughter *confidential?"*

She just said "I live *the impossible dream* and I am *the great pretender.* I have had my share of *lonely teardrops* and I have written many *love letters in the sand* to my *little darlin'* who is a *long gone daddy.*

Now you know a bit about me, do you want to tell me something about you?"

He thought about it for a short while then said "You're right about me *searching* for something and someone. When I was younger I travelled a lot too. *I've been everywhere; I've* travelled all *around the world* on a *surfin' safari.*

I went to the *surfside* of Jamaica and as *the boys* and I were leaving, we got a traditional *Jamaica farewell* where the citizens call out "*let there be drums* and let the *mission bell* ring."

We went to *wonderful Copenhagen* but Hawaii is a *wondrous place.* It is really the *island of dreams* where you could have what the people called a *hula love.* I have been on many *trains and boats and planes* and yes, I was a *wild thing* for many years. I remember when I was in Hawaii, hearing about the sinking of *THE HUCKLEBUCK* but at the time I was too interested in *hangin' five* from my board and listening to the *rhythm of the rain* on the roof of my bungalow at night.

I was in *Surf City* when I met *Tammy,* a local girl. She would tell her friends "*he's my blonde headed, stompie wompie real gone surfer boy* and she would also say that *he's my boy lollipop.*"

We went out together for a while and every morning when she came round, she would greet me with *good morning star shine* and when we were out on the surf, she would say *hi ho silver lining* just before a wave dumped her. It was like surfin' on a *sea of love* with her, but one day I heard the *Hawaiian wedding song* and *the clapping song* and I found out that it was her getting married. So I came back home and met *Peggy Sue* who was a *party doll.* She told me one day that she didn't love me and went to a party with Eddie.

I lost everything in those few years, so I took to the road hoping to find what I was looking for. *I live for the sun* at the moment because *there's always something there to remind me* that *if I only had time* I might be able to forget and let go of all the hurt I still carry."

Molly said "I understand what you mean, but you can't *keep on running* all your life and keep telling yourself that it's *oh lonesome me* and *I just don't know what to do with myself. Only you and you alone* can find the *little boy lost* inside you and bring him home. Sometimes you just have to *cast your fate to the winds* and *begin the beguine;* sorry, I meant to say begin again; if you don't let go of *yesterday;* then tomorrow won't come along and you could be spending many more nights in the *Heartbreak Hotel.*

It's hard for me to accept that my *little bitty pretty one* has now grown to the age of wearing *lipstick, powder and paint* and becoming a *runaway*. I'm glad that both girls haven't much money because it means that they couldn't catch a *night train* to somewhere that would be harder for me to trace them. I knew which way to start travelling because *Lorraine, runaround Sue*'s sister was *shakin' all over* when she was *at my front* door and *just one look* of her face told me something was wrong. She told me that she had just seen Sue and Lucille in the cabin of one of the *Tequila* Company's *Six-Five Jive* trucks heading out of town.

I went to the *Tequila* Company and found out that the driver, *William Tell* was *the man from Laramie* and was on his way back home via *Tobacco Road,* so he would have had to come this way before turning off just before *Blueberry Hill,* another twenty miles down the road. He would have had to stop here and if the girls were heading somewhere across the States; then they would have to find another ride from the *Sugartime* Roadhouse."

Ah!! There is the *Red River Rock* junction just ahead. We'll stop at the roadhouse, I need to get more gas in the car before I travel any further and we can also get a meal. I don't know what way I'll be going next because I will have to find out if Lucille has been here."

A MAGICAL PLACE

As Miss Molly pulled into the roadhouse and up to the pumps, Bobby noticed that it was also another truck stop. Red River Rock was a small town; a few houses, a post office but a town just big enough to have a hotel. The roadhouse itself had a few rooms built onto one side of a diner, which looked like it was also part of a small shop. A *hound dog* was chained but sleeping near the entrance of the shop.

As she stopped, a man who had the build of a grizzly bear and the features of a Red Indian came over to attend the gas pumps. When she got out the car and turned around, the man said with delight "*Good golly Miss Molly*. What brings you way out here? I haven't seen you for years. How are you doing?"

With a surprised look on her face, she looked at the man and said "*I remember you; Running Bear*. Hello. Yes, it has been a long time and *I'm doin' fine now*. Could you fill her up with gas please? How are you doing?"

I'm married now and have *seven little girls* and there's another on the way. I hope it's a boy this time." said Running Bear. "You park your car and come inside for a bit so you can meet the family and tell me what brings you so far from your home in the big smoke."

Bobby was already out of the car and he turned as he heard another truck pull to a stop and someone yell out "*Hello Josephine.*" He was surprised to see that once the woman had alighted from the driver's seat that she was a really *little bitty pretty one* and wondered how she was able to handle such a big truck.

She walked past Running Bear who asked her "*Hello Josephine.* Did you get the mechanical issue with *Do Wah Diddy* solved or are you driving *Sha La La?*"

Josephine answered "Yes, *Doo Wah Diddy* was fixed by *Bo Diddley* at the *High School Confidential* Truck Garage in *Bongo Rock* and now she gives me *good vibrations* and not the *shake, rattle and roll* that I used to get when I drove her. On a *school day* Bo teaches mechanics to some of the *sweet little sixteen* year old students and in school vacations, he allows his students to still work under his supervision on vehicles; especially trucks, because Bongo Rock is predominately a truck town. Allowing the young ones to work during their vacation and earn a bit of cash doesn't allow them time to get the *summertime blues* and get into mischief. Bo bought a vintage truck that the kids call *Splish Splash* and together they are restoring it for the town's truck museum."

Miss Molly parked the car and then they all went inside. The inside of the diner was decorated with Indian Artifacts that made you feel welcome and in front of one exhibition was a sign that read; "*Please Don't Touch The Merchandise. Please ask the staff for help. Thank You.*"

Running Bear poured them all a mug of coffee and put a plate of *ginger bread* in front of them and Miss Molly explained her situation with Lucille.

"Wait a minute, I'll go and get my wife, she may have seen her in here." said Running Bear as he slip through a doorway to the back of the store.

He was only gone for a moment but while he was gone, a little girl went riding through on a stick pony crying *giddy up a dong dong,* then he returned with his wife. He introduced her to both of them then Miss Molly introduced Bobby to them.

Then Running Bear said "*Don't you know Yockomo.* We were going together the last time we met at the beach. She was with *Lady Godiva* who was modeling an *itsy bitsy teeny weeny yellow dot bikini* for the *Three Steps To Heaven* Magazine. We both knew at the time that *we've gotta get out of this place* so we packed up and started driving. We stopped here and asked *short fat Fannie "Is this the way to Amarillo?"* Fannie was elderly and had a For Sale sign on the front window of the shop and we bought the place. *For what it's worth;* we have built it up and we love the place.

In the beginning, Yokomo was a *tower of strength* and a *good luck charm* for me when I wanted to move on, but now she has me doing the *blue jean bop* because there's no other place that I would rather be at, than here with my family."

Yockomo said she thought that she saw some girl fitting Lucille's description talking to the truck drivers last night and she would go and ask them about her. When Yockomo returned she said that the drivers remembered her and another *runaway* girl named *Runaround Sue* trying to get a lift to *Memphis Tennessee. Runaround Sue* said that they wanted to see this guy named *Charlie Brown.*

The drivers don't usually give hitch hikers lifts but *Beatles Medley* decided to give them a lift seeing that he was passing through Memphis.

25

Before they left, he said to one of the other drivers "They look like *sweet little sixteen* girls and if I don't take them, then they may *flip, flop and fly* with some *sixty minute man* who may give them the *summertime blues* and doing them harm."

"Of course." said Miss Molly "She's trying to get to her uncle's place. My brother, *Charlie Brown* who is a few years younger than me and believes *rock and roll is still alive*. He would even rock and *roll over Beethoven,* his *hound dog*. She feels that he is her *hurdy gurdy man;* the one she could tell her troubles to and he would *make the world go away* for a few days. When *you're sixteen* and *singing the blues;* who would she turn to if she needed to talk to someone other than me? I should try to give him a call so he will expect her. That is, if she hasn't already rung him."

Yockomo asked if we would like a meal and a place to stay for the night. She said "Not many people drive through these mountains at night because the *long and winding road* that passes the *Mountain of Love* is dangerous if you don't know the terrain.

When Running Bear and I first came here we already knew *what a wonderful world* we had, but in this place we seemed to be like *strangers in paradise*. We went up to *Wolverton Mountain* and made *love on a mountain top* and had a *wonderful time up there*. We stayed there until the fog lifted around *high noon* the following day and when it did, *suddenly there's a valley,* a beautiful piece of earth to *look out* at and the *Moon River* flowing through a part of it to a large blue lake.

It seemed to me that *cloud lucky seven* with a special *hi ho silver lining* was hiding *my blue heaven and the sun will shine* on my life for quite a few years to come. It was one of those *magic moments* for me and the next magic moment for me was when my *angel baby* was born because she had *pretty little angel eyes*. I have seven daughters and they were all born with the same kind of eyes and that is why I call them *my special Angels*. I think that this next baby will be a boy.

I am a descendent from the Chickasaw tribe; the Chickasaws were living in villages in what is now Mississippi; the area around *Memphis Tennessee,* and were hunters and gatherers. Both Running Bear and I will do everything we can to make sure that our children know of their heritage so that they can pass it on to their children and grandchildren. *I believe* that the Great Spirit created this earth and everything and everyone on it and above it. Soon after moving here, we found that many a *supernatural thing* would happen but it didn't faze us because of our traditions and beliefs."

While Yockomo was in the kitchen cooking their meals, Miss Molly went to try to phone her brother and Running Bear was in the shop serving customers, Bobby looked out the window and thought he saw a male disappear twice behind a tree that stood *solitaire* from the others.

Yockomo returned with their meals at the same time as Molly did and Bobby told Yokomo what he thought he saw and she said "You just saw our *Earth Angel* David. He is *my special angel* because when you see him you know that *love is all around.* He will *put a little love in your heart* and will talk to *Venus* who will do the rest. *I say a little prayer* for *this magic moment* to *wake up everybody* who has the *lovesick blues.* If you ever see a *blue moon,* look to the right and you will see the *blue star.* Make a wish and then say *"give me love."* You should get some *good vibrations* when you're in the company of your next love. You know *it takes two to tango* but there *ain't nothing like the real thing* when it comes to love."

Running Bear came back in and stood beside his wife saying *"The Garden of Eden* is everywhere around you and all you have to do is open your eyes to see its beauty. *I get around* a lot less now, but when I do have to go away on business, I know that *the most beautiful girl* in the world to me is waiting here for me back home. *I found a love* many years ago and I work on it every day so that we will always be *happy together* besides *I'm dedicated to the one I love* or rather I should say the ones I love."

Yockomo looked at Running Bear and said *"For your precious love* I would go and *catch a falling star,* just to give it to you."

Yokomo excused herself when they all heard *"Hey, hey, hey, hey. Don't ha ha me* about *my blue suede shoes. You're breaking my heart again* because of that *lipstick on your collar. Do you love me* or not? Don't answer that because I already know the answer. *Oh boy, you send me the yellow rose of Texas* and it ends up being *poison ivy.* Now *hit the road Jack* and don't ever bother me again. *It's all over now* and I am going back to my *pistol packin' mama* if you're game enough to come around."

Then they heard "This ain't lipstick *little darlin';* it's a blood stain from cutting myself shaving last week. When you said *baby let's play house,* I thought that you wanted to *come on over to my place* but *Lawdy Miss Clawdy* all you want to do is fight so now I'm saying *bye bye love* and

I'm walking. Go back to *mama* and go *flying saucer rock 'n' roll...* you know what I mean Miss *la dee dah.*"

Running Bear looked at Bobby and said "I didn't need to go in because just the sight of Yockomo going in there has stopped the fight. No-one who knows my wife is game enough to continue fighting in front of her; especially those two.

Carrie Anne was once a *high class baby* who became a young *calendar girl* for *Raunchy* Teens Magazine but when she became *breathless in the still of the night* after blowing out her *sixteen candles* on her *birthday* last year, she was rushed to hospital where they found that she had contracted a different strain of the *rockin' pneumonia and the boogie woogie flu.* The strain that she has affects her brain and can give her the *mean woman blues* and everybody knows that if she's had *no milk today,* then they don't talk to her.

Stagger Lee; well, *he's a rebel* and thinks that he's just a *lovin' machine.* He'll tell you himself that "*I'm a moody guy* with an *itchy twitchy feeling* and will *flip out* if you don't do what I want when I want."

We can't really stop them from coming in, but we make sure that they don't stay for very long."

Customers started coming in to the shop so Running Bear left to attend to them.

After returning Yockomo spoke *sincerely* when she added "On *such a night* like this *I see the moon* and I know that *the lion sleeps tonight* with the *tiger* in a cave near where the *Moody River* meets the *Moon River in the middle of nowhere.* The *pretty Flamingo* and the *Mockingbird* will sing together in the morning and the *Honeysuckle and the bee* will together give us honeycomb. The Great Spirit has said that *it will stand* as such until *the end of the world,* then *look homeward angel* as we will be waiting for you.

It may be just *sentimental me* talking but I think that, that *stupid Cupid* is at work again and will *speak softly love* words for all those who need to hear them. Oh; I should warn you that *there's good rockin tonight* after the main evening meal is over."

After they had finished their meal and Molly had, had some *Peppermint Twist* ice-cream, Bobby said to Miss Molly "*Do you wanna dance?*"

28

She replied "*Slow dancin' don't turn me* on but you can *rock me baby* so *come on let's go* out on the floor."

Running Bear came over to the table after they had finished their dance and said "*Scarlet O'Hara* will be *singing the blues* tomorrow and asking everybody "*What'd I say* to you last night 'cos I don't remember after drinking all that *Tequila* last night."

Scarlet O'Hara approached Bobby and said "*You're so square baby, I don't care* but will you *come go with me* to the floor and dance with me?"

He looked at Molly hoping that she would object and save him but all she said smiling was "*Be my guest.*"

As he got up to dance with Scarlet, he looked back at Molly with pleading eyes and asked "Will you *save the last dance for me?*"

Molly looked back and still with a smile on her face said "Yes."

Yockomo, who was cleaning the table beside them, whispered in his ear just before he got up to dance with Scarlet "*The night has a thousand eyes* and they will *ambush* you for *your precious love* if you are not careful. *All you have to do is dream* of love and *no one but you* can let the ambush happen. Love will happen in time and it will be *sealed with a kiss.*"

The rest of the evening passed quickly before they decided to retire for the night.

THINKING BACK

As he did every morning, Bobby woke early, dressed and went to the diner to wait for Miss Molly to come for breakfast. He had just started on his first cup of coffee when she arrived but somehow she looked different. He thought "*What in the world's come over you?*" then he asked her how she felt as she sat down.

She replied "I feel *Wonderful! Wonderful!* How about you?"

Bobby said "I'm not sure. *Something's got a hold on me.* I feel as if I could *shake rattle and roll* then *rock around the clock.* I can't really explain it. I feel as if I have been *born free* again. I feel as if there has been a great *exodus* of all my *sorrow* and hurt."

"*Goodness gracious me,* I know what you mean. My heartaches and sorrow just seemed to *slip away* during the night and I don't feel like *someone broken hearted* anymore." said Miss Molly "*Rock on rock and roll and let's dance.*" And then she thought "*Gee whiz look at his eyes.* I have never noticed that they were such a beautiful shade of blue, loving and tender and he has a great *personality.* I could make you my *dream lover* and *all I have to do is dream* to get you close to me."

Yockomo came over and said "Good morning. You two look *happy together;* like *two lovers* who have just discovered each other. I noticed that there was a *blue moon* last night and I thought about you seeing *Earth Angel* David and *I wonder* if he has *bewitched* the both of you in a good way. *What'd I say* to you last night Bobby, about the strange things that happen around here. Molly, would you like to order now?"

Miss Molly blushed and said "Yokomo, *please don't tease.* I am just giving Bobby a ride down the road." and gave her order. She then thought "*I like it;* I like the feelings that I have now. Last night must have been the first time in years that there were no *tears on my pillow* before I went to sleep and no *tear drops* on my cheeks this morning when I woke." It was hard for her to *try to remember* the last time she had felt like that.

Bobby had already placed his order but waited for Miss Molly to join him.

They finished their meal, said goodbye to Yockomo then went outside to say goodbye to Running Bear who was talking to *Petite Fleur,* his second daughter "The Great Spirits say *don't be cruel* to animals or your fellow man. Now run along before *Mr Custer* gets annoyed with you being late for class again."

Running Bear turned to Molly and said "Once you've driven through the mountains, go through the next town and stop at the next one, *Jambalaya*. Go to *The Happy Organ* Motel and *Mr Blue* will look after you. His wife is *Long Tall Sally* and she makes a refreshing, reviving drink called *Breathless*. Take care and call in if you happen to be out this way again. I hope you find Lucille."

Molly said "*Thank U very much* for your hospitality and I'm sure that I'll find my daughter and *runaround* Sue safe at my brother's house."

They were both very quiet when they started down the road again as if they were both deep in thought; which they both were.

He thought "*Hey there lonely girl, I'd love you to want me. With a girl like you* to *rescue me* from *endlessly* searching for a place to be where my heart will be wanted would be great. *Oh, lonesome me*, do I want to be *the wanderer* going down *Tobacco Road* for the rest of my life.

He then remembered again when he last saw *Peggy Sue* and how she was a *party doll* and the last conversation that they had, had.

He had said to her "*I know you don't love me no more* and all you want is a *finger poppin' time*. All you want to do is *rock on rock 'n' roll*."

To which she replied "You're *just like Eddie,* you're like a *rubber ball* that I can bounce at any time I want. Why don't you go *knock on wood* and just *keep on knockin'*."

As she walked away he said "*That'll be the day* when I am sitting here waiting for you to say *I'm sorry* to me, and never again will *you keep me hangin' on. You always hurt the one you love* or loves you. *See you later, alligator;* go and have some *good rocking tonight* and *since I don't have you* to worry about anymore I can get on with my life."

Then he said "You had better get *ready Teddy* because you will be her next victim. She may be a *pretty woman* but her *promises* are venom which is much worse than *poison ivy*. Her venom will *not fade away* quickly, so don't listen to her *sweet nothings* or you'll end up like me and her other loves; suffering *the summertime blues* all year round. The other guys that she was involved with all ended up crying *please please, please don't leave me*, but she ignored them and now they're *singing the blues*."

She turned to the other guy and said "Don't listen to him. Are you *ready Teddy? It's my party* tonight so let's go and have some fun down at the *Great Balls Of Fire Club*."

31

Then he heard her laughing reply she was walking away "Who cares, I don't. Oh; by the way, all the flowers you sent me were just like *poison ivy* so I threw them in the trash and all the other guys were like you; not good enough for me."

"She was *bad to me* so I left the *little town flirt* and now, *I who have nothing* have become a wanderer. *Somewhere my love* is waiting for me and I want *a sweet old fashioned girl* to love and *hold me*." he thought.

Molly thought "Jones, *I can't stop loving you* but maybe *I've been loving you too long* and sometimes I have played *the crying game* over you, but now I think it's time for me to play *the game of love* again.

Earth Angel will you be mine and *I can't help myself* but I want to become *Bobby's girl*. Please don't let *lightnin' strikes* take him away from me.

Jones, *baby what do you want me to do?* Please *gimme a little sign* if you think it's time for me to let go of you. I have had enough of being *the great pretender*."

Molly turned on the radio just in time to hear "*Unchained Melody*." and she knew it was a sign from Jones to her to let him go. Bobby, should I *tell him* about the sign from Jones?

Molly's thoughts were interrupted by a bad section of road. It looked like the road crews that were parked on the side of the road were ready to *rip it up* and resurface that section.

As soon as Bobby heard the song he immediately tried to remember what the Australian Indigenous elder from the *Mony Mony* tribe had said about him hearing the music in time, and how love would be around or something in that fashion.

Both the Australian Indigenous people and the American Indians have a belief in their culture and their ancestral stories. They also believe in the spirits of the land and of the sky so I had better listen to the stories that I have been told by them. They may not be right in everything but it won't hurt to keep an opened mind. I think that there are quite a few more cultures that have the same or their own beliefs, customs and stories passed down from one generation to another that they still believe in.

They drove through the small town of *Jailhouse Rock* where they saw a sign that said "*It's my party,* at the park so come and join me." but the *rhythm of the rain* kept them going and they stopped at the place that Running Bear had suggested in *Jambalaya*.

It had stopped raining by the time they had reached the outskirts of Jambalaya. It seemed to take until *the twelfth of never* to find The Happy Organ Motel where Running Bear had suggested that they stop for a break. As they both got out the car, they both looked at each other and smiled and said in unison *"Let's go in."*

Sitting in the doorway, they passed two small boys talking about the *Christmas alphabet*.

The first little boy said "Last year, *I saw mommy kissing Santa Clause* and when I told daddy all he did was laugh. He didn't even get angry with her. When *it's Christmas time again* and if I see mommy with Santa, I'm going to get daddy so he can see her with him."

The other boy said "My *mamma loves papa* but I have heard them talking at night when I am supposed to be asleep.

One night I heard papa say to mamma *"What now my love.* I think that we should contact Susie and find out what she wants to do?"

Then I heard mamma say *"Hello Mary Lou,* could you *wake up little Susie* as we have some bad news to tell her." Mamma was quiet for a moment and then she continued "Lulu went on a *sea cruise* on the *Que Sera, Sera* but *the cruel sea* put her in an *endless sleep.* Please *come back, Maybellene* needs you here."

The first boy said *"Gee.* Was she *lost* in the big ocean for very long and will you miss her?"

"Nah." said the second boy "Lulu was the pesky dog next door and she was on Seakka Lake in *the boat that I row* sometimes. A storm blew up and with the wind *blowing wild,* it turned the boat over. The man who was rowing the boat was *okay* but the dog disappeared and I won't miss it one bit. *Maybellene* is the girl next door and it was her dog."

Right said Fred, "Now off you go; your mothers are calling the pair of you."

33

CHASING LUCILLE

They entered the motel's reception area where a man was sitting behind the desk and as he stood up, Bobby noticed that he had what looked like a *goldfinger* on his left hand.

"*Mr Blue.*" Bobby said "Running Bear recommended we stop here for a break and one of your wife's refreshing, reviving *Breathless* drinks."

"Oh yes, Running Bear, he is a good friend, but all those children he has. He must take *Love Potion No 9* to keep up his stamina. Are you wishing to stay the night or are you just going to dine?" asked Mr Blue.

Miss Molly said "We haven't decided yet. Do you know how far it is to *Memphis Tennessee* please?"

"Well, we are *halfway to Paradise* and Memphis is that distance again so I would say about another 100 miles." said Mr. Blue. "Maybe you would like to rest a bit over a drink before you make up your minds. My wife *Long Tall Sally* will look after you in the restaurant." he added.

They walked through a small café that was a bit smokey, to the restaurant and went in. The restaurant was decorated in an elegant *James Bond theme;* like one would find in a big city but it had a notice just inside the door. "PLEASE BE SEATED. TABLE SERVICE ONLY THANK YOU".

Miss Molly sat down and wiped her eyes and said "I couldn't sit out there because the *somke gets in your eyes,* and with all that *yakety yak* going on, it would drive me insane. I would also have to *shout* for you to hear me."

Long Tall Sally came over and introduced herself then recognized Miss Molly and said "*Good golly Miss Molly. I remember you* and I haven't seen you since high school but *I saw Linda yesterday. Shirley Lee, Diana, Donna* and *April Love* were in here the other day. They were going back to San Francisco after spending a *white Christmas* and a few months in Canada with *La Bamba.*

Diana told me that *La Bamba* hasn't changed much, because she still works in the *Raunchy* Construction Site food halls and that is mainly *where the boys are.* She also said that the boys *walk right in* for a meal at any time during the day. You know that her real name is Paula Bamballa.

Donna continued "It was a *beautiful Sunday* and Paula's day off so she took us sight-seeing and while we outside the *Aquarius Music* Shop, a male approached her and said "*Hey Paula,* you've got *ole man trouble* again. *Mack the knife* has just been kicked out of the *Pretty Flamingo* Movie House again because he was making too much noise through the *Roll, Hot Rod, Roll* movie. You know how excited he can get during those types of movies."

We left her to go and sort it out after she said softly "*Oh mein papa make* my life easier and take your medicine on time. *Please Mr Postman;* bring me that letter from the home that will take *the weight* of caring for you off my shoulders." *Ain't that a shame* because she really is so smart and she has to spend most of her time caring for her father because of his illness."

The last time I saw all you girls together was *at the hop* before we all graduated and went our separate ways. Although I *love Mr Blue;* Trevor, very much *I left my heart in San Francisco* when we moved here; however, my *little darlin'* has allowed me to make a few changes to this place and it has become a very popular place for travelers and locals alike to stop, rest and eat. Do you remember the girls and will Jones be joining you soon?"

Miss Molly said "*Great balls of fire,* why does everyone keep calling me that, my name is just Molly? No, Jones won't be joining us as he was lost at sea sixteen years ago."

Trying to change the subject, Molly asked "Have you seen two young girls in the past couple of days looking for a ride to Memphis? One is a *runaway* named Lucille and the other one is known as *Runaround Sue*."

"No, I haven't, but maybe they were in the café. If you wait a minute, I'll ask the girls out there. *Jenny Jenny,* have you seen two young girls looking for a ride to Memphis? One is a *runaway* named *Lucille* and the other one's name is *Runaround Sue*."

"Yes." said Jenny "They are both with *Alley Oop*. He's a good truck driver so they'll be safe with him. He had a load for *Mr Lee* and a couple more companies in Memphis on board. Harlequin, you know Mr. *Don't Ha Ha Me* who drives the *Don't You Rock Me Daddy-O* rig; DYRMDO rig was going to take them but he has to detour to a few other places first and thought it wouldn't be good for the girls to be travelling all that way with him.

They were with Beatles but he had to make a detour to *Twenty Flight Rock* to pick up an urgent delivery from the *She She Little Sheila*

Company, so he left the girls in the care of Alley. They should have reached Memphis the day before yesterday."

Long tall Sally replied "How do you remember all the truck drivers' names, nicknames and the rigs they drive? *That'll be the day* when I remember just a quarter of them."

"*That's alright*. I know them because I have more contact with them than you do. You know most of the regular customers in the restaurant and I don't." replied Jenny.

"Yes and *Jenny takes a ride* to *Jingle Bell Rock* with *Maybelline* when she is in town. It's good that cousins can get together throughout the year, but fancy calling a big rig like she has, *Matchbox*." said Mary Rose.

As it was early afternoon, Bobby and Molly decided to go for a walk around the town and down to the *Yellow River* that the town was situated on. The walk would be good after all the sitting down they had done in the past few days and they wouldn't be *just walking in the rain* as the clouds had disappeared and the sun was warm. They finished their drinks then slipped out another door instead of going back through the café. Molly said that she should park the car in a more suitable spot.

As she walked away Bobby thought "There goes a *Venus in blue jeans* with a light blue *Chantilly lace* top. If she was my girl, I would *take good care of her*. Hang on; does this strange feeling I get when I'm around Molly mean that I am falling in love with her? I know that I told myself that *when I fall in love* again it will be with an old fashioned woman, but Molly is also an honest woman and will never let me play *the fool*."

Molly returned to him and they both walked down to the river where they found a man-made beach complete with lots of sand. Molly picked up a stick and wrote *love letters in the sand* then brushed them away with her hand.

Bobby sat on the *Arkansas grass* where some *autumn leaves* had fallen from a tree. She gave Bobby *just one look* and he saw the *sorrow* in her eyes.

He thought "*Oh pretty woman;* what is it that is making you so sad? You are *the great pretender* but you will have to stop pretending and *lay down your arms* one day and I want to be the one who helps you to *walk right back* to a happy world. I can tell that *you've lost that loving feeling* but right now; *who do you love* and *what do you want?*"

They only stayed a short while at the beach, and then they walked through the town.

Molly noticed and said to herself "*He walks like a man* who is just like *poetry in motion*. He is a *living doll* and with *just one look* from those *dreamy eyes* I could melt into his arms and *stay* there forever."

Molly stopped in front of an Ice-cream Parlor and said she was going in for some *Tutti Frutti* ice-cream.

While she was in the parlor, Bobby slipped into the shop next door and when Molly came out of the parlor he handed her some flowers and said "*Red roses for a blue lady.*"

Molly took the flowers and said "Thank you. *Little things mean a lot* to me." then she thought "You must be an *undercover angel* to make me want to love again. No-one else but Jones has made me feel this way before. I must be falling in love with you because I've *got to get you into my life* and *I'm gonna make you love me?*"

Then two young people came out of the parlor and the boy said to the girl "*Jesamine* please *tell Laura I love her* and ask her to *save the last dance for me* as I'll be late getting to the *Jailhouse Rock* 'cos I don't finish work till late. Tell her that *Wooly Bully* and *Sheila* will be there early tomorrow night and he will be teaching *The Locomotion* and *The Twist*. If you tell her, then she can let me know if she wants to meet up when I get there and where we shall meet. There will be a new band called *Sun Arise rockin' the joint* and I have heard that they are very popular in *Surf City.*"

Molly had changed into a *deep purple Chantilly lace* dress with a *honey* colored shawl wrapped around her shoulders and all through the meal Bobby thought "*I can't take my eyes off you* and *I'm gonna make you mine*. This afternoon you were my *Venus in blue jeans* and tonight you look beautiful. I wonder what would happen *if I give my heart to you?*

During their meal Molly heard long tall Sally say "*Ramona, you're sixteen* so you shouldn't be in here unless you are with your parents."

The male said "*Say mama, turn me loose*. There's gonna be a *whole lotta shakin' goin' on* in here tonight and we want to be part of the action because you have to *rock on rock 'n' roll*. We promise that we'll stay away from the bar and behave ourselves."

The girl said "*When the red red Robin* wants to dance, we usually do.

We're gonna rock around the clock and it will either be in here or in the café. Please let us dance in here on the dance floor. *If you don't know me by now* and know that you can trust me then; we'll leave. The *Jailhouse Rock* Hall is too crowded to be able to dance properly and I would like to try out my new *blue suede shoes* on a decent floor."

Sally replied "I shouldn't let you in but I do know you and if you *try me* and my patience or cause any trouble or go anywhere near the bar, then it won't only be me that you'll have to deal with; it will also be your parents as well. I will make sure that you have enough water on your table to drink throughout the night."

After their evening meal, Bobby asked Molly if she wanted to stay and have a few dances.

Molly's reply surprised Bobby when she said "No, not really. For some reason I don't feel *in the mood* for dancing and I would rather just have a quiet evening with you."

They went for another short walk *in the misty moonlight* down to the *Moon River* Lagoon that was nearby; keeping right away from the *Jailhouse Rock* Hall. Upon returning to the motel, Bobby said goodnight and was about to walk away from Molly who was standing at her door.

She thought to herself "*All I have to do is dream* to have you near me tonight but *why* should I so *he'll have to stay.*" then she said "So I don't need to *sleep walk* over to your place, please *stay* and *come softly to me* as *I need your love tonight.*"

Bobby was surprised by what she had asked and thought "*Ain't she sweet* but *what do you want to make those eyes at me for* 'cos you already have me." and then replied "*I don't know why but I do* also need your love tonight. We can talk *sweet nothin's* to each other tonight but *will you love me tomorrow?*"

"There is *something about you baby* and are we starting to talk the *language of love*. Is this the beginning of a new, *young love* or are you going to take me up to the last *three steps to heaven* and then *release me* and end a short *love story* by walking away? Please *don't be cruel* and *don't go breaking my heart* leaving me with *tears on my pillow*." he thought.

He walked up to her and took her hand as she opened the door and they went inside. She laid her head on his shoulder then said "Oh dear, I have just put some *lipstick on your collar*."

A GREAT DAY

When Molly woke the following morning, she found herself alone in the room. Bobby was nowhere in sight. She laid in bed reminiscing over what had happened the night before. "*It's only make believe* that he could love me. *It's just a matter of time* before *he will break your heart.* I guess that this is the after effects of our night in *Red River Rock,* being so close to the *Mountain of Love.* Yes Jones, *I'm in love again* and I'm *not responsible* for the way I'm feeling.

You used to *hold me, thrill me, kiss me* but the *cruel sea* took you from me so many years ago and *all alone am I* now. Yesterday I wrote you my last *love letters in the sand* but I still carry your last letter with me and if I need to talk to you *all I have to do is dream* and we'll be able to talk. *It's my life* and I *can't help falling in love* with him because *it's in his kiss.* I will always love you but in a different way now but *please love me forever* in the way that you used to do." she thought.

She realized that there was a *knock on wood;* someone was at the door. Whoever it was *would keep on knockin'* till she answered it.

When she opened the door, she saw Bobby standing there holding *eighteen yellow roses.*

He said "*Hey baby.*" as he walked into the room. "I don't know how you feel today, about last night but *I'm telling you now* that *I love how you love me.* I know that it is new to both of us but if *we walk – don't run* we will be fine. Oh *don't let me be misunderstood* by what I just said; I mean that if we take it slowly then our love can grow stronger as we really get to know each other better.

For me *it's now or never* to start loving again and *my prayer* for someone to love me as much as I love them may have been answered by you. Yes; I was badly hurt by another person years ago and I was in Kansas City searching for someone, but it wasn't *till I kissed you* last night that I realized that I have found the one I wish to be with and *baby it's you. Anyway that you want me* for now will be alright by me but there is one thing I do know and that is *I'll never find another you.*"

Molly stood and looked at him stunned for a moment then said "When I woke this morning *you were on my mind* and when you weren't here I thought that you were gone for good. *Baby, now that I found you,* I think for me it's *too late to turn back now.* I feel like *a teenager in love again* and that I could do the *ABC boogie* all over this room.

Jones will always have a special place in my heart but *you're so fine* and I want you for *my own true love.* I never realized it *till I kissed you* last night that *maybe baby* you are the answer to *my prayer,* and *it's now or never* for me as well, to see if our love can grow. *Please Mr. Mayor, hold me now* and *kiss me quick* before I come back down to earth and have a chance to change my mind."

Bobby turned and gave her a pat on the backside and said "Get ready and let's get out of here and this time I'll drive so you can have a rest today. If we can get back on the road soon, we can make *Memphis* by late this afternoon and you will see *Lucille* again."

They were back on the road an hour later and before long they pulled into Paradise for a quick snack and to gas up the car. Bobby bought a *lollipop* for Molly to have in the car because she seemed a bit jittery as the passenger.

During the last leg of their journey, Molly was starting to feel nervous about seeing *Lucille* again so she turned the radio up a bit more. Bobby gave her a reassuring glance and then Molly thought "*As long as he needs me,* I will stay with him because that glance of reassurance made my *heartbeat* race a little."

Then over the radio the announcer said "*Don't knock the rock* but this is a new style of song to listen to." and he played the song *A Lover's Concerto.* Both Bobby and Molly looked at each other and smiled. It was going to be their song.

They drove into Memphis before dark and found *Primrose Lane.* Molly said "That's my brother's house, the one with *the green door.*"

Bobby parked the car, got out and they both walked up the path hand in hand and Molly nervously knocked on the door. She was hoping that she wouldn't have to *keep on knockin'* because she felt like she was *shakin' all over* with the excitement of seeing her brother again after many years away and nervousness of being reunited with her daughter. How would her daughter react in seeing her mother again?

A *hound dog* barked around the side of the house as a man with a *baby face* opened the door. He looked at Bobby first then he said "Molly, come in, we've been expecting you."

"Charlie is she here?" asked Molly concerned.

"Come and meet the family and then we'll sit and talk. Please excuse *this ole house* as it was our parents place before they were killed in a plane crash. I've been trying to renovate it but time is always against me. I have been thinking of employing some of *Willie and the Hand Jive* Carpenters or *The Magnificent Seven* Handyman Service to help me but I'm not sure what the cost would be." said Charlie.

Molly introduced Bobby and said lovingly "I am now Bobby's girl. Where's Lucille?"

They walked through the house to where the back garden was. He introduced them to his wife Rosemary then said "*Love grows where my Rosemary goes*. And these are my *little children,* this is *my girl Josephine* and the girl playing with the dog, Beethoven is *Corina Corina* come and say hello to your aunt Molly."

They all went inside the house where Rosemary made coffee and they reminisced about old times.

Charlie said that when he first saw Rose she was working in a club named the *Sha La La La Lee* and went by the name *Rose Marie*. At the time, she was like a *rambin' rose; a painted tainted rose,* that looked like she needed *the Garden of Eden* to bloom in. He said that he used to wonder, *where do you go to my lovely* when you are not at work? *Never on Sunday* was the club open so what was she like then, a *party doll* or a *paper tiger*.

Then he looked lovingly at her and said, "Remember that day when I was *just walkin' in the rain* down *on the street where you live* and you came out of your front door. We bumped into each other and we started talking. Not long after that we started dating and then you suddenly disappeared for a while. When you came back you said to me *sorry I ran all the way home,* so quickly that I thought my feet were like the *wings of a dove.* I looked around and saw a rose bush and thought "*I'll pick a rose for my rose.*" and I did and gave it to her. Now she wears my ring."

"Yes, I remember." said Rosemary "You also said that *roses are red my love* and *remember you're mine* for as long as you want to be because *memories are made of this.*" and then she said looking at Molly "*If I knew you were comin' I'dve baked a cake* this morning. We thought that you would be here tomorrow. I tried to work out last Tuesday just how long it would take you to drive here from Kansas and I had *Friday on my mind* as the day that you would arrive."

Charlie said that Lucille was out and would be back shortly. He said that since the girls had arrived he had, had a good, long talk with them and that *Runaround Sue* would be going home in a few days after talking to her parents.

He also said that Lucille said that she felt like she was tied to her mother's *apron strings* and that she also felt that her mother just existed as she no longer had something or someone to live for, and that she didn't matter to you anymore. The suggestion of *let's have a party* was made because they both knew that you liked to listening to and dance to music that was a good *foot tapper* but *you've lost that lovin' feeling*. The reply that you gave the girls did a *wipeout* on a *young girl* who was only trying to get close to you again and make you happy.

I think that you have a *story untold* to tell Lucille and it's about time you told it. Molly if you don't; then you'll *keep searchin'* for your *runaway* until she can no longer be found by you. Your past with her will *not fade away* until the story is told and she understands *why* you kept it from her."

Molly became *all shook up* and a *tear drop* rolled down her cheek by what her brother had just told her. "I never knew that Lucille felt that way." said Molly "we have never really sat down and talked. I found it very hard to explain the real reasons for her father not being there for her when she needed him.

"I became *the great pretender* to cover up my secrets from my daughter but I also covered up the best part of my life from people; the best part being my daughter, my *sunshine girl*. *The little shoemaker* on *Surfside* corner, *Mambo Italiano,* knew about Lucille and how I felt and he told me to *walk don't run* as she grows up. He told me *don't let go* of my dreams and that I can have it *all or nothing at all*. I didn't really understand what he meant until Lucille became the *runaway* again and the events that have taken place on this trip to find her.

I knew that *one fine day* I would have to tell her but I was never *ready, willing and able* to do it. I was going to take her to the beach where Jones and I first met and during *the stroll* along the water's edge I was going to tell her about her father and the *story of my life* after our parents died and I left here. Now I think it's *time* I *stood up* to my fears and tell her, but still I don't know how to do it without giving her the *summertime blues* or getting *the ballad of Davy Crocket* thing that the teenagers give these days when they don't want to listen."

"Molly." said Charlie "After our parents died and you took off; I had many *tears on my pillow* over things that were out of my control.

Tequilla and drugs became my friends for a while and then I met Rose and it took me nearly two years to tell her about my past.

I got sick and came down with a bad *fever* in *Hernanto's Hideaway* and Rose bought me home and *at my front door* she told me that she would *stand by me* and help me sort my life out. It has been a struggle for both of us but we have done it. Love grows when you can share your troubles and know that *walking back to happiness* is possible with that special person beside you.

Lucille may get mad and not want to talk to you, but she may be just the opposite, and will want to help you to *walk right back* to a happier life for both of you. Give her a chance and now you've got Bobby here to support you. I suspect that you have told him about some of your past."

LUCILLE'S STORY

Molly was on edge while waiting for Lucille to return to Charlie's house, so much so that she got up and walked out to the back garden so that she could try and get her thoughts in order. As she sat under a tree where Charlie had placed a park bench, she thought "*Oh boy!* What have I done and what have I become in my daughter's eyes? How are we going to work this out? What will I say to her? Now, what about Bobby? I don't want to lose him but how will he take this? Will he stay?"

Tears started to fill her eyes when Bobby approached her, sat down beside her, took her hand in his then said "*Little darlin'* don't let this become a *blue Monday*. When Lucille gets back, talk with her and *tell it like it is. The girl can't help it* if she has been unable to get *close to you*. She has the *teen beat* in her so don't *tighten up* if she starts asking questions or gets upset."

Molly looked at him and said softly "What about you?"

Bobby put his arm around her and said "*Hey baby, put your head on my shoulder* and listen to me. *If you don't know me by now* then *ain't that a shame*. You know that *my heart is an open book* and that *only you and you alone* will be the one to help me write the empty pages with happy times and memories."

The back door closed with a feint bang and both Molly and Bobby turned their heads to see Lucille walking towards them. Bobby got up and walked inside, leaving Lucille and Molly alone.

Lucille said "Mom, I'm *sorry I ran all the way home* when Uncle Charlie phoned and said you was here. I was doing the *baby sitting boogie* with three children for the lady down the street but I couldn't leave them *alone* so I had to wait until their mother got home.

Uncle Charlie and I had a long talk when I got here and I didn't understand what you had been through; losing your parents in a plane crash, then having me and then losing my father at sea all those years ago. I can see why you didn't want to talk about it but you should have said something when I got old enough to understand and then I could have tried to help you get through of your bad times. You would always *come softly to me* when you thought that I needed to talk or just needed a hug."

Lucille added "Who is that guy? He seems nice."

"That's Bobby." said Molly. "We have known each other for a couple of years when he lived in *Kansas City*. He left about a week ago and we met up again a few days ago on the road while I was looking for you. Something happened to both of us on this trip and I think that for the first time since your father died I am falling in love again. Yes, he is a very nice, gentle man.

Baby, now that I've found you I want us to work things out because *every time you go away* I just *wipe out* a bit more. I feel lost and Lucille, I am sorry for not being the mother I should have been to you. *I'll make it up to you* if you'll let me."

"Mom, I am no *teen angel* and I may be a bit of a *wild one* but *I love the way you love me,* anyway what was that saying Uncle Charlie always said when you got down, "*rock 'n' roll is still alive* and so are we."

Mom before we go in, could we talk a bit please?" asked Lucille. "I found out that Sue got called *runaround* Sue because she used to help her mother look after elderly or sick people and she used to *runaround* and do odd jobs or run errands for them. People say the runaround part is because she hangs with a load of male friends.

Sue spoke on the phone to her friend and said "*Hold on, I'm coming* and I will most probably hitch hike as I can get there quicker. Don't worry I'll be careful." With me being unhappy because of what was happening at home, I decided to *runaway* with Sue who wanted to come here to support a close friend of hers, Ginny, whose sister is very ill.

The experience that I had travelling here opened my eyes to a lot of things. In the Red River Rock Roadhouse, a woman and a young man were talking and the young male said "But *mama, he treats your daughter mean* and you intend to do nothing about it?"

The woman got up from the table and said "It's time to *hit the road Jack* and if we *move it* we can be home before dark. Your sister's situation has nothing to do with you and there is nothing I can do for her until she comes to her senses. He has *too much* of a hold over your sister and *I say a little prayer* each night and hope that in the morning *that'll be the day* that she will be asking herself "*Where did our love go?* and leave him and come home."

Then when Sue and I got here Uncle Charlie spoke to us about the dangers of our leaving without telling anybody and hitch hiking. And then after he had spoken to us separately, I realized that I had been very selfish in my actions many times.

I knew that you had a secret that you wouldn't tell me but I didn't think about how you felt. I still don't think that I'll ever understand what you went through for all those years; it's just like trying to understand what it was like and in some ways still like for Ginny and her relatives.

Ginny and her family are descendants from the Afro-American slave trade. Her first relative to come here to America was a paid servant but when his contract was finished, his employer would not let him leave his service or go back home to his family so hence he became a slave.

An outbreak of Yellow Fever happened about ten years after his arrival due to the poor sanitary conditions and the mosquitoes that bred in the dirty conditions around where Memphis was first settled. One white family's members that attended to the sick people on a barge that was towed to Memphis also became sick and the disease spread through the whole town and many people died from it. People fled from Memphis so they wouldn't get the disease but it spread to other towns and cities as well.

Yellow Fever seemed to affect the white people more than the Africans. Evidently in the African people, they carry a hereditary blood disorder called Sickle-cell disorder or Sickle-cell anaemia which helped quite a few people to have immunity against Yellow Fever and Malaria. Ginny's little sister *Gigi* has been diagnosed with Sickle-cell anaemia which means her blood cells are not like normal ones but are curved and can cause blockages in the arteries that keep the organs working properly. It is also a hereditary condition passed down from generation to generation. I would love to learn more about it and I think I will.

To keep her mind occupied when she is unwell, Ginny plays her sister a lot of music; Gospel and Rock and Roll. Their mother told us that in the late forties and early fifties, the white people started singing the black gospel music in a faster beat and that is when Rock and Roll began. Did you know that entertainers like Nat King Cole who had their own television show were the only dark skinned people on their show? It was very hard for them to get sponsors for their shows so they had to work under white management. I think that's what she said. Even today, the origin of most of all of American music is from the African culture.

Even though the Civil War brought about the freedom for many slaves in Tennessee, they still had to live in a segregated society. It has been a harder struggle for Ginny and her parents and relatives to be accepted because of the colour of their skin. I personally think that to see a person on a skin deep level is wrong; you should look past the skin and find out what's inside the person. If a person is good or bad then that's what you will find out.

Living in Kansas City is a lot different from living here. There is a guy back home in our *sweet talkin' city* who often says *sweet nothings* to me but I know that he's *only lonely* and wants people like me to like him. I will talk to him but that's all I would do because he is too old for me and we don't really have much in common.

Come to think of it, I always thought that the Blues, Jazz and rock and roll was music written by white people and I never knew that another culture from another country could have anything to do with it; especially when the songs have a great *melody*. I wonder, what would we do without music?

I like it here mom and I wish that we could move in here with Uncle Charlie for good. I know that I could get some *baby sittin'* to help us out until you can get on your feet. Mrs. William's said that I could look after her *Susie darlin'* anytime. She told me that after I left last time, she gave Susie her *teddy bear* and Susie gave a little squeal and uttered *nee nee na na na na na nu nu;* her first *baby talk* noises. Mr Johns asked me yesterday "You *take good care of my baby* so are you available to look after *Mandy* again next Tuesday afternoon for a couple of hours please?"

I'm sorry mom for not being a good daughter. Will you forgive me? Come on, let's go in. I want to meet this Bobby of yours. He seems to have a great *personality* and is like *poetry in motion*. Am I right?"

Molly blushed and smiled then said "Yes, I also think the same about him. Lucille don't be sorry as you are not a bad daughter; just someone who didn't know all the facts. In years to come I don't ever want you to *be my life's comparison,* because you have to make and lead your own life. *You're sixteen* almost seventeen and *you're my world* but *the games people play* in this world can have you being *the wallflower* listening to the same old song like it is on repeat. You can be *somethin' else. You got what it takes* to be anything you want to be. Remember that.

I grew up here remember, so I wouldn't have to think hard about moving back here and being closer to my family but I think that we should discuss it with Bobby first, don't you?"

Molly and Lucille went back inside and sat down with the others and then Molly said "We have sorted a few of the most important things out, and together we will work on the rest from now on."

Charlie said "Molly, you know *this ole house* is big enough, so you can all stay here, until you decide what you want to do in the future. Only the renovations may be a bit of a problem."

"Maybe I can help you there." said Bobby. "I was a *handy man* in *Kansas City* and since I have *no particular place to go* I could give you a hand. *If I had a hammer,* nails and a saw I could start helping you if you want me to."

"That would be great." said Charlie gratefully. "The renovations will take some time because this ain't a *doll house* you know."

That night Molly took Bobby up to *Blueberry Hill* and Bobby laid out a *crimson and clover* colored rug for them to sit on. Molly looked horrified when she saw the rug but Bobby said to her "We will forge a new ending for this rug; not the one you remember." As they looked up, they both saw a blue moon and Molly said to Bobby *"Do you love me?"*

Bobby said "Yes, I do. *I love you because* you're so gentle, patient and you have a great heart amongst other things. *I only wanna be with you* and I want you to always *get lost in my arms.*

Molly, I *gotta see Jane,* she's my sister; she's a *calendar girl* designer and I want to tell her about us right away. She lives in *Bombora,* a suburb of Phoenix. Tomorrow I'll go to the *bus stop* and catch the bus there and that will give you some time alone with Lucille. This will be the last time I'll be *on the road again* alone and *by the time I get to Phoenix,* you and Lucille should have been able to get closer."

Just before Bobby got on the bus he looked Molly in the eyes and said *"I'm a road runner today* and I'll be home before you know it. Remember *I only have eyes for you* and *you're my world* so *as I love you* so much, will you be *my baby* and wear *this diamond ring?"*

With great surprise as Bobby put the ring on her finger, she said "Yes. *With all my heart I love you baby. Lover please* hurry home and keep safe."

The following evening a story came over the news that said a bus bound for Phoenix was hit by several *lightnin' strikes* down by the *Pipeline* Junction. A couple of passengers were killed and many of the others had been injured.

Molly sat in shock and thought "Oh, *don't you just know it; the story of my life* is happening all over again. Somebody please *tell me when* I have to stop *singing the blues. Stupid Cupid,* why did you have to do this to me again?"

Charlie immediately went to Molly while Rosemary changed the radio station.

Molly thought of Jones and then the next song started playing, it was *Unchained Melody;* the song that was a sign from Jones for her to love again. Was this another sign or is it just my wishful thinking that he's okay?

The phone rang and Lucille answered it, and after a brief conversation with the person on the other end of the phone said "Yes, I will do that for you and then *mama* it's for you."

A NEW FUTURE

As Molly got up to go to the phone she thought "*Here it comes again,* bad news just like all those years ago." then she saw a small smile on Lucille's face and thought hopefully "*It must be him.*"

"*Hey Baby.*" said Bobby "I heard the news story and knew that you would be going *crazy* thinking that you could have lost me the same way as you lost Jones, so I rang you straight away to let you know that *it's alright;* it wasn't our bus.

I have talked to my sister and I have told her about us. I told her *that you were made for me* and *she wears my ring* now because I'm going to give her *all my loving* and I hope that she will *love me forever. And then I kissed her.* At the moment *all I have to do is dream* of you and *I feel good* like I'm a *teenager in love* for the first time.

Phoenix is now a city of *tar and cement.* My sister is married now and her *mother-in-law,* a *Kentucky woman* was once Miss *Sugartime.* It is raining here at the moment but *without you* here *it might as well rain until September. Gee* babe, I miss you and *only the lonely* would know how I'm feeling right now. *I'll be home* in a few days. I am going to fly back with *Telstar* Airlines so I can get back to you quicker. Now, you remember, that from now on *you'll never walk alone. You're my world* and *you made me what I am today. You got what it takes,* so *I'm counting on you* to keep being the *tower of strength* that I know you are. You know that *I love you baby. Goodnight my love.*"

With tears in her eyes Molly said "I feel like *a hundred pounds of clay* has just been lifted from my heart. *Since I don't have you* here, please *come softly to me* in my dreams and let me hear *all sweet nothin's* in my ears; like the ones you've said to me before. *For your precious love* I will have to wait for a few more days and now I know that you're alright I can do it. I love you too so *goodnite, sweetheart, goodnite.*"

Bobby said "*Well I'm your man* and we'll be *walking back to happiness* together. Would you please put Lucille back on?"

Molly handed the phone back to Lucille and accidentally overheard Bobby say to her "Now you *take good care of my baby* for me and we will get to know each other better when I get back. That is if you want to."

"Yes I'd like that." said Lucille then thought "He really is a nice man and *he'll have to stay* with us." as she hung up.

Molly was so relieved to hear that Bobby was alright that she was just about to go into the kitchen to make a cup of coffee, when over the radio came an announcement "This is *dedicated to the one I love* and you know who you are, then the song A Lover's Concerto began to play and she knew by the look on Lucille's face that Bobby had asked her to get the station to play it for him to her. Molly thought back to the time at Red River Rock. How Yokomo had told them about Earth Angel David and how he will put a little love in your heart and talk to *Venus* to do the rest. Thank you David; you are now *my special angel.*

"Daddy, daddy, come quick." cried a little girl's voice

"*Corinna, Corinna.* What is it, what's wrong?" replied Charlie as he rushed into the family room.

"Look what I've just taught Beethoven to do. Come on now, *roll over Beethoven.* Good boy." beamed Corinna.

Rose, Lucille and Molly also went rushing into the room thinking that something was wrong only to be greeted with Corinna saying "*Let's do it again, roll over Beethoven.* Good boy."

Rose walked over to Corinna and gave her a hug and said "You are a very clever girl to be able to teach Beethoven to do a trick like that after all these years. Now, off to bed as you have a big day tomorrow. *Goodnight my love* and don't forget to say good night to your father and our other guests."

After both Josephine and Corinna were settled in bed, the rest of the family sat talking and Molly and Charlie started reminiscing about their younger days and their friends.

Charlie said "Do you remember Louie who used to *knock three times* before he walked through a door. Well, he worked at *the House Of The Rising Sun* until there was an explosion in the kitchen and the *great balls of fire* burnt the whole place down one night after they had closed.

He also played the drums in a band because he had learnt to play them as a child living with his grandparents in a Chickasaw village in what is now Mississippi; the area around Memphis Tennessee.

He was *walking after midnight* with their singer, *Georgy Girl,* taking her home after the gig had finished, when they happened to notice smoke coming from the direction of the restaurant. As they reached the end of the block, they saw the flames and called the fire brigade.

They knew that they should not go near the restaurant because it could be dangerous if *smoke gets in your eyes* or you can get *breathless* by inhaling too much smoke so they just had to watch the building burn. He now works for *Mr. Lee* in his catering business as one of the chefs."

Molly's reply was "*Louis Louis Young Blood.* I remember that he tried to change his last name because he was always being picked on at school. I also remember that he would tell people "*I'm a moody guy* so *don't knock the rock* if you don't like the music." I believe that he only said that to keep people away.

I can't remember if it was *Gloria* or Georgy Girl who had a crush on one of the teachers and would often enter the classroom saying "*Hey baby,* I'm here so it's *to sir with love* for a period of time."

Rosemary interrupted them by saying "*I remember you* taking me out one night to a show at the Orpheum Theatre, but when I saw the white people going in through the front door and the Afro-Americans going around the back to get in; I thought that that was so disgusting.

You know that I used to slip out and go down to the end of Beale Street just to listen to their music which I found was uplifting. Now I know that thanks to their music, *rock 'n' roll is here to stay.*

One night when I was down there, Blake Birch caught me standing against the wall listening to the music and came over to find out what I was doing there. A couple of minutes later Miss Troublemaker came walking past slowly and Blake said "*Hello Mary Lou.*" and then *he kissed me* to make it look like we were out together. He then said "*I get around* and I know that Mary Lou will say something if I turn up at the *Jailhouse Rock* tonight on my own so *do you want to dance* and *come go with me?* I'll make sure you get home safely.

I thought that if *I pretend* to be with Blake then everything will be all right but as soon as we had walked into the *Jailhouse Rock,* Blake walked over and said with a smirk on his face "*Hello Mary Lou; all alone are we?*"

Mary Lou looked him straight in the eye and replied "*What'd I say* to you last week at the *Locomotion* Amusement Park to make you say *bye bye blackbird* to me? You know that I'm *hopelessly devoted to you* and I *cry* for you because *I only have eyes for you. How am I supposed to live without you?"*

"*Ya Ya. Have mercy baby.*" said Blake "*I'm a man* and I am not going to be *the leader of the pack* of males who you can say *sweet nothings* to, *shake a hand* with and leave when you have had enough. I saw you go into that *Honky Tonk* place with your little two legged *hound dog* following you or should I call him your lap dog. I have noticed that *when you dance* to *the Banana Boat song,* you look like *poetry in motion* and can leave a man *breathless,* and when you give them *a certain smile; they long to be close to you* and think that *we will make love.* You end up leaving and them saying "*There goes my baby* but why, what have I done or haven't done?"

"What did you expect me to do when I saw that *lipstick on your collar* and I heard you tell Evan "*Tell Laura I love her*." yelled Mary Lou.

"*Hey there;* it is not acceptable for you two to carry on like that in *here and now*. Please, take it outside if you want to carry on and neither of you will be allowed back in if you are in an angry state." said a big tall man as he walked over.

Somebody tapped me on the shoulder and I turned to see a friend standing there.

"*Hey Jude,* it's good to see you." I said

Jude looked at me and said "*Come on let's go, it's late.* I've got to get you out of here because you're *all shook up* by that incident. *What in the world's come over you?* I saw you walk in with Blake and you know that he's bad news. Oh don't bother to *answer me* now. I hope that it won't take you long to stop *shakin' all over* otherwise you'll have a bit of explaining to do to your parents when you get home."

I never went back down there to Beale Street again although I missed the music that I heard and loved. In fact, I rarely went out, except to go to work after that because I never wanted to run into Blake or Mary Lou; that is until you came bumping into my life. After we had been dating for a while, you used to often give me a red rose saying "*Roses are red my love.*" and you still say that when you give me one."

"*When a man loves a woman,* he'll do whatever he can to make her happy. *Your love keeps lifting me higher* every day and *because I love you* so much and *because you're mine;* I want to always *take good care of my baby.*" said Charlie lovingly to his wife and then he turned to Molly and asked "Molly, we have only known him for a short time so please tell us about Bobby?"

"Yes." said Lucille "I would like to know more about him. Has he told you much about his family and where he grew up?"

Molly thought for a moment and then said "I only know that he was a handyman in Kansas City and he lived in a small apartment block. He told me that he travelled a lot in his younger days. He told me that he went on a worldwide surfing safari and he did odd jobs to earn the money to keep travelling. I only found out on the way here that his last name is Mayor and on our first night here, he told me that he had a sister, Jane who was a *Calendar Girl* designer. I have no idea what a Calendar Girl designer does and that her mother-in-law is a Kentucky woman who was once Miss *Sugartime,* but he has never mentioned any names except for his sister's name.

He hasn't told me anything else about his family, where he was born or where he grew up. He also gave me this expensive ring and told me that he was flying back here in a few days. I think that it's good for him to have time with his family but I hope that he hasn't had to get some work to pay for his plane ticket. Now *I wonder where my baby is tonight;* is he at home with his family or is he working?

When he gets back here, I think that I will have to have a very serious talk with him and I hope that he will *answer me* truthfully. At the moment I feel like a *stranger on the shore* of a very deep lake that I have agreed to jump into with him."

Lucille looked at her mom and said "Mom, now don't start doubting your *dream lover*. I think that the deep lake that you're talking about is really the *Sea of Love* and you're scared that you will get *hurt* again. Maybe there is a good reason why he became *the wanderer* but he seems happy now because he has found his *dream girl*. *I wonder* why he hasn't really told you much about himself considering he has asked you to marry him. I suppose that all will be explained when he gets back here but if he is still very secretive, you'll have to make the decision if you still want him around or if *he'll have to go*.

I'm going to go to bed as I will be taking *the stroll* down to *The Three Bells* Ice-cream Parlor tomorrow with *Diana, Peggy Sue,* Josephine and Corinna. I promised my cousins that they could have a *Peppermint Twist Tutti Frutti* cone each and Aunt Rosemary said that it was alright.

Good night everybody and mom; Bobby would say to you before you go to bed "Don't forget to *dream a little dream of me* tonight and *since I don't have you* here with me I'll do the same."

MEETING NEW FAMILIES

Molly stood staring out of the lounge window thinking about Bobby when Rose walked up and stood beside her and was just about to speak when a cab pulled up outside and Bobby got out. He was talking to someone else who was still sitting in the back of the cab.

The person came into view and Rose said surprisingly "I know her. That's Jane Trimble; the most sought after fashion designer. She has just celebrated her tenth wedding anniversary to the top horse owner in the country. *I wonder why* Bobby is with her?"

Molly replied "Well we'll soon find out."

Bobby came through the door excited as if he was about to explode. He took one look at both the females and said to Molly "*Hold me.* I have some good news that I want to tell you. Is Lucille here as she should hear this as well?"

"No, she has taken Josephine and Corina down to get an ice-cream cone. She is also with two other girlfriends so I don't expect her to be home for a while."

Bobby looked at Rose and said "When will Charlie be home?"

"He arrived home about half an hour ago. Why?" asked Rosemary.

"Could you go and get him and come to out to the back porch please?" asked Bobby.

It was a matter of a few minutes until the four of them were sitting on the porch with drinks in front of them.

"As you know Molly, I went to Phoenix to tell my sister about us." said Bobby. Molly shook her head yes and then Bobby continued "Whilst I was there I was able to look into a few things and one of them was getting a permanent job so that we could settle down once we were married."

Charlie looked at Bobby and said "Rose said that you came home in a cab with another woman. Is that right?"

Rose was just about to continue when Charlie said "*Honey hush.* Let him explain."

Bobby said "Yes, I did and I hope you don't mind but I have invited her here to meet you all and she'll be here any minute now.

Charlie, I hope you got the front door bell fixed or *she'll keep a knockin'* till someone answers. Ah! There's the door-bell now. Don't get up, I'll answer it."

Bobby walked back out to the porch and said "Molly, Rose, Charlie; this is my younger sister, Jane. Jane is also going to be staying at the Grand *Hula Hop* Hotel up town for about a week as she intends to do some business here."

Bobby looked at Molly and said "I needed to know that *the girl that I marry* would love and want to marry me for who I am. Over the years it always seemed that *somebody stole my gal* because I wouldn't always give them what they wanted. I didn't let on who I really was because I knew that they would only stay with me for my money, but with you I know that *I'm into something good* because *I love how you love me* for who you thought I was.

Molly, I'm asking you again; will you marry me and take me as I am even though you don't know much about me at the present?

Instantly Molly replied "Yes. I will because *I'm stone in love with you.* See, it's *because I love you* so much that I can't even answer properly."

Charlie let out a loud phew and said "I think I need another drink; maybe a *Tequilla*. Anyone else want one?"

Bobby continued "*I need you now* to know the truth about me and my family and that is why Jane is here as well.

My full name is Bobby Mayor-Brodhead and I am from Louisville Kentucky. My sister and I inherited *the Da Doo Ron Ron* worldwide chain of general stores and clothing emporiums when our parents split up. Jane went to live with mom in Lexington Kentucky where she attended the University and graduated with honors in designing. A few years after that she married Trevor Trimble but she still continued to work as she enjoyed the challenges. In the beginning as she was getting started in her business, she worked under her maiden name and shortened it like I did; however, these days she goes by her married name.

Dad was never interested in what I did so I took off with some friends of mine and we went on a worldwide surfing safari. Gradually the guys left and went back home but I hooked up with some different guys who didn't know who I was. It was fun being with them and I used to enjoy doing the odd jobs here and there; even though I didn't need to work. I also enjoyed meeting different people and learning about their culture.

When I came back to America, I tried to settle down but it didn't work because I had too many *tears on my pillow* from my past.

Molly; *do you want to know a secret?* You were one of the reasons why I left Kansas City.

I had seen you around town and on a couple of occasions we spoke *sweet nothin's* to each other for a few moments but one day, I saw you *crying in the chapel* and I just wanted to go over to you so you could *put your head on my shoulder* and cry there. Another time I bought you some flowers and had some *red roses for a blue lady* but I was afraid that you wouldn't accept them, so I gave them to an elderly lady instead and that made her day.

The night I left Kansas City you were with another female watching the Chefs cooking over the *great balls of fire* before she asked *"Do you want to dance?"* I knew that *I only have eyes for you* and *don't you just know it;* I still *can't take my eyes off you* and *I only want to be with you.* I often wondered *why do fools fall in love* like I had, and *who do you love* so much that it's breaking your heart? They say that *big girls don't cry* but I know they do; especially if they think no-one is watching.

The craziest thing is; *it had to be you* who I ran into while *I'm walking* down *Tobacco Road."*

Molly looked at Bobby and said "Remember when Yokomo said *"I see the moon* and I know that *the lion sleeps tonight* with the tiger in a cave near where the Moody River meets the *Moon River* in the middle of nowhere." and some other things; as well as "it may be just sentimental me talking but I think that that stupid *Cupid* is at work again."

I think that he was at work and working with *Venus* because *I'm a believer* too and *you are my destiny.* All I know is that *I'm in love again* and *you were made for me."*

Young female voices were heard coming up the drive and Charlie said "Ah! The girls are home. Now you can meet my daughters Josephine and Corinna and Molly's daughter Lucille."

Lucille called out "Corina, what is it with you today? It seems that *I only have eyes for you* at the moment or you'll just disappear. Next time I go for ice-cream, I might take Josephine with me and leave you at home."

Corina replied "I said that *I'll come running back to you* if I didn't feel safe; and anyway we're home now so you don't have to worry about me."

Once a bit more chit chat was exchanged between the girls and their parents and after Rosemary had made some afternoon tea for them all; Josephine and Corinna went to play in the garden and Lucille was asked to join the grown-ups because what Bobby had to say from then on would also concern her.

Bobby looked at Jane and whispered "Here goes." and then "I have been offered a position with a company here in Memphis but I have not accepted it just yet. I needed to talk to you all first as it would mean moving and settling down here in Memphis.

Charlie, I know that it's awkward with all of us here and not being able to get the renovations done so if it alright with you, I would like to pay for *Willie and the Hand Jive* Carpenters to come and complete them for you. It would take you twice as long to do them *if I had a hammer* and was helping you.

Rosemary, would you discuss this proposal with Charlie and let me know as soon as possible please so I can book them in if you decide to go ahead.

Molly and Lucille, I would like you to think about and discuss the option of moving here to Memphis permanently. I know that there are some very good schools, colleges and universities here that Lucille could go to. Not to mention the friends that she has made all ready."

Molly and Lucille looked at each other and then Molly said "*Charlie Brown, I'll be home* again as soon as I can get my things from Kansas. I feel like *I'm a tiger* at the moment and I just want to become the *leader of the pack* and get everything done quickly. Both Lucille and I have discussed it and we want to move back here but we were going to discuss it with you first Bobby."

Jane pulled a folder out of the bag that she was carrying and said "Charlie, Bobby tells me that your company makes clothing materials. Is that right?"

Charlie nodded yes.

Jane continued "This is my latest swimwear design and I was wondering if your company would be able to come up with the material to make it with this design. It's an *itsy teeny weeny yellow polka dot bikini* and the emphasis is on the dots being very small but noticeable. We didn't want the yellow to be too bright so we have come up with a *mellow yellow* colour that suits the design.

58

I am also looking for some different ideas for a dress or wrap to go over or around the bikini; so if you know of anyone who could give me some suggestions, then that would be good as well.

Raunchy is going to make a beach bag, hat and slip on to go with it but if I can find a manufacturer around Memphis I would like to talk to them about making and supplying the accessories for me. They would have to be in the quality range of *Raunchy* but in an affordable price range for the customers to pay."

Rosemary said "The *Proud Mary* Accessory Company might be the people to talk to about that. Their products are very popular down here in Memphis and the surrounding counties and they are reasonably priced."

Jane continued "My husband and *my little drummer boy;* my son Troy, will be back at the hotel later on today and we would like you all to be our guests at the *OB-LA-DI, OB-LA-DA* tonight. Trevor took Troy on a *mystery train* ride today so that I could do some other business and come here.

The *OB-LA-DI, OB-LA-DA* is an outdoor restaurant where the chefs cook your meals on hotplates over *great balls of fire*. The food has a great smokey taste when it's served and the best thing is; that you don't have to dress up to go there. The restaurant owner is a man named *Mack the Knife* and he comes from Kansas City. He also serves up a drink called *Love Potion No 9;* and has a non-alcoholic version for the younger ones. After the food has been eaten, they roll out a dance floor; so *let there be drums* and *let's dance* the rest of the evening away."

Bobby looked at Molly and said "I wonder if that's the same *Mack the Knife* that we know?"

"If it is, I know what he will say about me when he sees me "Molly, she's my *little bitty pretty one* and usually *she wears red feathers* in her hair when she goes out dancing." He always called that because he said that I reminded him of his *little darlin'*.

He would tell me "*My gal is red hot* and will *love me tender* when I get home. I travel a lot in my van that she named *Hi Ho Silver Lining* because the back section is lined with stainless steel to keep all my cooking equipment clean and properly stored in while I'm driving. We had a *merry Christmas* on the road one year and she surprised me by hanging *silver bells* from the saucepan rack. She can *send me some lovin'* anytime but it will be even better if I'm home."

Jane stayed for another hour to discuss her brother's new position and then went back to her hotel.

As soon as they arrived at the hotel, Jane was waiting for them with her secretary; she whisked Bobby and Molly into another room where she had some papers to be signed immediately by both of them.

Jane turned to her secretary and said "*Take a letter Maria.*" and then dictated it to her. "Please forward a copy of the letter to our lawyers with these papers. Send a second copy to our head office with these papers and a third copy with these papers to our new company here. When you have completed those tasks; *wake up little Suzie* and join us for an evening of fun and laughter."

It took Molly a fortnight to pack and freight her belongings from Kansas City to Memphis where Bobby and Lucille were waiting for her. Bobby had flown her there and back to save her time and the driving that she would have had to do.

Bobby had started his new position as the second in charge of the *I Walk The Line* Fashion House. It was a store where customers of any age and sex could purchase the fashion clothes sold in other stores and fashion boutiques for a lot cheaper without compromising the quality. The main idea of opening a store in Memphis was mainly to target the young ones in to buying the latest big city fashions and this is where her new bikini line was going to be released.

Jane had intended to start the new fashion store somewhere in the States and encourage the local businesses to make her fashions for her. It was perfect timing for her when Bobby turned up and told her about his engagement and coming marriage to Molly.

He had also mentioned that Molly didn't know much about his past and thought that he was just a wanderer. Molly grew up in Memphis and they would be staying there with her brother until they had worked out where they were going to live and where he was going to work. He had to also think about Lucille and her education and getting her settled so that she wouldn't want to run away again.

LUCILLE'S PARTY

It was about a month later when Bobby came in and said to Molly *"I've been a bad bad boy*. Well, Charlie and I are both bad boys because we both said together *let's have a party;* so we have just arranged to have one, but it is going to be a surprise party for Lucille. We have spread the word around to *the young ones* and told them it will be held at the *Waterloo* Stadium Hall next Saturday. *We're gonna rock around the clock, twist and shout,* and do *the Locomotion*. Well, what do you think?"

Molly looked at him and said *"Um um um um um um,* I suppose it'll be alright. Have you arranged music, food and drinks for them? And what did Rosemary say?"

"Yes, everything has been taken care of. Rose said *that's all right* with her. Now all we have to do is get through the week without Lucille knowing it's for her."

Lucille came to her mother and asked "Mom can we talk please?

I don't know why but I do really like Bobby and I know that you love him. I didn't know my real father at all so I don't know how you'd feel if I started treating Bobby like he was my dad. We have had many long talks and I respect him plus he has given me many things to think about and one thing he did tell me, was to *think about tomorrow* today and I think that really makes sense."

"I am very *proud of you,* especially for supporting me when I thought that I had lost Bobby, and I would be happy if you wanted to treat him that way. There are *sixteen reasons* for me not wanting to stop you. Have you spoken to Bobby about this?" replied Molly.

"No. I was hoping that you would be with me when I spoke with him as it really does concern the both of you." said Lucille.

"Darling, *what do you want from life now?"* asked Molly. "You know that some things you have to work and sacrifice for and I can tell you that it's *easier said than done*. Sometimes things happen and then you search *endlessly* for a reason or a solution. *You're sixteen* and *you never can tell* what is going to happen or where you will end up in the future. It's good to have goals but first start with small ones and build up to the big one so that you can reach them easily or to be able to work out a different strategy to reach your goals if life takes a turn on you. But let's talk about it some more tomorrow, it's getting late and that party is on tomorrow and *it's almost tomorrow* now. Go on off to bed, goodnight."

Bobby made sure that they were running a little late for the party. When they arrived they heard *1 2 3* and shouts of surprise. Lucille looked at her mother, who looked at Bobby, who then said "It's your party. I know that you have always wanted one so Uncle Charlie and I have arranged this one for you."

Lucille walked into the hall saying "*It's my party, it's my party*. Thank you. *I've waited so long* to have my own party and it isn't even my birthday. Look there's *Lily in pink, Donna,* Anna-*Marie Marie* Traverse and *hey Paula* is even here."

Looking around Lucille turned to her mother and said "Ginny's not here. I hope that *Ginny come lately* sorry I meant that I hope Ginny comes later on."

Bobby replied "She will be here later and we have arranged for her to be picked up after her mother gets home."

Someone yelled out "*Let there be drums* and let's *dance with the guitar man*. Sorry, there will be no *Ode to Billie Joe* tonight. Come on *rockin' Robin* and *rock your baby*."

Robin was with *Sheila,* who had just broken up with Johnny, but no-one knew why. *The finger of suspicion* was pointed at *La La* Johnson as she had always wanted to be Johnny's girl. Johnny was the *son of a preacher man* and was very popular, especially amongst the girls.

Someone asked "Who will dance with Lucille?"

"*Johnny will.*" came a reply.

While they were waiting for a different song to be played, Johnny asked Lucille how old she was and she told him.

"*You're sixteen.*" he said surprisingly "Well, you're a *sweet little sixteen* so let's go and do the *sweet little sixteen twist*. This floor will be good to *dance on little girl* since you have your *blue suede shoes* on." as he took her hand and walked her to the dance floor. As he was walking her through the different groups of people he said "*Wake up little Susie* and let us through. We have to *let the little girl dance*."

"I don't really like the way he's talking because he makes me feel like *I'm just a baby* and I should really *dance with a dolly,* and not him. I think that I should *tell him* that I don't like the way he's treating me." thought Lucille.

Later that evening, Johnny asked Lucille if she wanted to get a drink and some fresh air and she said "Why not."

While they were outside, Johnny started to turn on his charm to Lucille and said "*Come a little bit closer* so I can rock you in my *cradle of love*. You are my *dream girl* and I am your *soul man*. It's our *time* to do some *multiplication*."

Lucille pushed him away and thought "*What am I doing here with you?*" and then she said to him "Who do you think you are, a teacher? No. I am not going to give myself to you and say *to sir with love*."

She turned and walked away from him, leaving him with a shocked face. "I don't think any girl has done that to him before." she thought to herself.

On the dance floor someone yelled out "*I got you babe* so *build me up Buttercup* and come and *bend me shape me* into a *paper sun*. *Tell Laura I love her* in her pink dress and I would like her to *save the last dance for me*."

Some young man walked up to Molly, but didn't introduce himself and said "*Mrs Brown you've got a lovely daughter* but she's a *mystery girl* because she has come back into the hall without Johnny. *I believe* that she has just found out what Johnny is like. He is only in it for *the good times*. *It's only make believe* to him and that the *young love* of every female will always be his to command. I wonder if each girl that he dates asks themselves "*Will you love me tomorrow* or will you find someone else?"

Then as the young man walked away, he saw Lucille and said "*Hey there* Lucille, will you *save the last dance for me* please?"

"*April Love, maybe tomorrow* we can get together." called out Johnny after coming back inside.

Lucille thought "I see what mom and Bobby meant when they said *memories are made of this*. Many times I have thought *let it be me* to become Johnny's next girlfriend but after what has just happened *that'll be the day* when I do. I think I'll just wait for *the real thing*.

I realize too, that when they said that *only you and you alone* have the power to lead your life in the direction that you want it to go; they meant it. There are *so many ways* that people can try to change your mind and thanks to Johnny *I'm ready* to start fighting them. I may not get it right all the time but *will you love me tomorrow* if I don't?

There is one thing I do know, that if that situation does happen, I will love myself tomorrow and so will mom, Bobby and the rest of my family."

Just as Ginny joined them they all heard "*C'mon everybody;* up on the floor to *twist and shout* and then we'll do *the Locomotion. Hey little girl, come a little bit closer* to your dance partner otherwise he'll have to *sleep walk* over to you to grab your hand to stop you spinning. That's right *Susie darlin';* just like *Reet Petit* taught you. Mary, if *you keep me hangin' on* for too long on the dance floor, *my babe* will have to come and *rescue me.*

What's that *Carrie Anne; let's twist again.* I intend to play something *for the good times;* for the oldies or should I say; the rockers who were dancing to these songs before we were even though of. I'll bet that when they were younger some of them could leave us *breathless* and saying "*How do you do it?* How do you *just keep it up* without a break? It wouldn't surprise me if a few of them could teach us a lesson because they could still dance now like they did back then."

The following day Molly received a phone call from Jane asking if Molly had her wedding dress and the bridesmaid's dresses already.

Molly stated that with all that had been happening over the past month, she hasn't had the time to think about it.

Jane asked "May I design and make your dresses for you please. It will be a Bridal shower gift from me as your future sister-in-law. If you have an idea on the style of dress and the colour then I'm sure we can make it to your *satisfaction.* I also have an idea for Lucille's dress and it will be something that she will be able to wear out at any time in the future. The design is from my collection that I called "The *Baby Love* Look" that I did whilst studying for my degree. I am sure that the style would be something that Lucille would like and would be happy to be seen wearing. Your dresses would be a one of a kind and if someone else decided that they wanted one; then the design would be slightly altered.

Molly stated "I was thinking along the lines of *blue on blue;* blue velvet dresses with a *Chantilly lace* jacket over the top but two different shades of blue. As for the styles, I don't have any ideas yet.

I think that I may need your help or I'll just end up going in my jeans because I couldn't make up my mind. Lucille would love for you to make her dress for her instead of me making it for her. Are you sure that you want to do this for me?"

"Yes, I'm sure. Anyone who can have my brother acting like he was *a teenager in love* again and very happy will always have my gratitude and love. It hit him very hard when our parents split up and to save a lot of hassles over Property Settlements; our parents signed over to each of us half of the companies and all the fortunes that went with them.

One night *at the Hop* that we were both at, he decided to *come softly to me* to tell me that he intended to leave and not come back. He told me that *my truly, truly fair* heart knew what he meant and why. He asked "Will *you send me* money from my account when I need it, without asking questions? *Only you* will be the one that I'll keep in contact with, so that you can call me if anything should happen and I need to come home immediately."

He went back to our father's place and packed a few clothes and left.

Only the lonely would know a part of what he went through because he had stopped remembering those *oh, happy days* that we shared and stopped *dreamin'* of the future. He used to send me the occasional postcard from where he was at that present time but I knew that he was very empty inside.

When he lived in Kansas City he phoned me and he told me about this particular woman that he would like to get to know better. The next minute, he is standing on my doorstep telling me about you.

He said "*I got a woman* and *she's so fine*. I left Kansas City because of my *secret love* for her and then *sh-boom* we meet while I'm walking and now *she's my baby* and we're going to get married.

THIRD STEP TO HEAVEN

The following day Molly, Bobby and Lucille went for a picnic where the *old rivers* met and Lucille talked to Bobby about what she had discussed with her mother the previous day.

Bobby said "That was *good timin'* because I wanted to talk to both of you. *Here comes summer* and *love is a golden ring* and if your mother will accept it, I would like to put a *band of gold* on her finger permanently. Lucille, *you send me* love and happiness as if you were the *dream baby* I never had, so I would be happy and proud if you would like me to be your father.

Now Molly, will you *answer me,* will you become my wife? Will you and Lucille be the ones to help me write the empty pages of my *book of love* with *magic moments?"*

Molly looked at Lucille and then at Bobby and said "*I will* because *I'll never find another you.* We will be proud to help you fill those empty pages."

"*Are you sure?"* asked Bobby.

"Yes I am. Maybe we could get married in the *Chapel of Love* and they can ring the *mission bell* afterwards. Jane has offered to make the Bridal Party dresses for us." replied Molly.

The rest day came and went quickly, so late in the afternoon; they headed back through town to Charlie's house. They went past a pet shop and Lucille stopped, looked in and said "*I wonder; how much is that doggie in the window?* I have always wanted a dog called *Ooby Dooby* but I couldn't have one in Kansas City."

That last statement made them all laugh.

"*Ooby Dooby* is not a name for a dog, especially for one with that colouring. *Honey* would be a better name." said Bobby.

Molly said "I don't think Charlie would appreciate us bringing another dog into his house. He already has *too much* going on and Bobby has arranged for the renovations to be started next Monday. With another dog running around, we wouldn't want it to be a *blue Monday* for everyone; now would we?"

Lucille replied "You're right. I guess *the lion sleeps tonight* on my bed again. May be one day I will be able to find out *how much is that doggie in the window* and then buy it and give it a home."

As they neared Charlie's house, a man approached them and said "*I'm the urban cowboy* and my wife is *Lady Godiva*. I have seen you around here for a few days now. Are you just visiting or do you live in this street now?"

Molly said "We are just visiting my brother, Charlie Brown, the family who lives in the house with *the green door*. I don't know how long we'll be here for, so I suppose we will bump into each other again."

The man replied "*Oh boy*. I *sincerely* hope that I don't have to *rumble* with you as well." And then he walked away saying "Now *I've got you under my skin* as well."

When they went inside Charlie's house, Molly mentioned the man to Charlie who said "He is the *semi-detached suburban Mr James*. When he and I meet, we get into such a heated discussion that Rosemary has to *soothe me* before I get too over heated. One of these days Rosemary won't be there and *that'll be the day* that I'll let him have it. Oh, I don't mean that I'll hit him but I won't back down and agree with him if I know I'm right and he is wrong.

We have just had a barbeque and there's plenty of food left over so *help yourselves* to something to eat. Rosemary has also baked *Honey Love* Twists without the extra *sugar sugar* that makes them too sweet. Rosemary makes them in such a way that they have just *a taste of honey* with a slight hint of ginger to them. We all love them so they don't usually last long."

All three of them had something to eat and then told Charlie and Rosemary the news of when they had decided to get married.

Charlie said to Molly "So you're finally going to be *walking back to happiness* again. *The weight* that you have had to bear by bringing Lucille up on your own will be greatly lifted. I think that you have done a really good job despite the circumstances you have had to endure. She may not have been a *little darlin'* all her life but she has grown into a beautiful and responsible young lady."

Rosemary said "Lately when *I get around,* I hear mothers telling each other that if they ever need a baby sitter then ask Lucille, because she will always *take good care of my baby* for me if I have to go out and she will take care of yours as well. I heard one mother saying that she is thinking of asking you for your permission for her to sleep over so that she and her husband can go to see the new play "*My September Love Lost John.*" when it comes out. Evidently they haven't been to the theatre since before she had her first *little darlin'*.

Do you need help with all the wedding arrangements because I could help you in some ways and *Mr Blue* could help in other ways? Do you have any idea of what you want to wear?"

Molly said that she and Lucille would wear *blue velvet* and *Chantilly lace* dresses with *blue velvet* ribbons in our hair but in different shades and styles and that Jane had offered to make them and..."

"And I'll wear my navy pants with *a white sport coat.* Would you be my best man Charlie?" interrupted Bobby.

Lucille said that she would wear her *blue suede shoes* to go with her outfit and that she would be able to dance in them afterwards.

Later that evening, Bobby walked into the bedroom and saw Molly looking at the last letter from Jones and she said softly "Goodbye Jones. *Will you love me tomorrow* because I'm getting married to Bobby*? I'm in love again* and *I like love* and the way it makes me feel. You told me once that you would *stand by me* and in many ways you have but now *there's no other* person that I want to be with except for Bobby. *I will follow him* to the end of the earth if I have to.

He saw me *crying in the chapel* after I lost you because I was in with the "*only the lonely*" crowd and now his is going to make me happy in the *Chapel of Love.* I loved you Jones but I love him *more than I can say.* I mentioned to you once about my *three steps to Heaven;* well you were my first step, Lucille was my second step and now Bobby is my third step. I knew God would get me that far."

She looked at the letter again as was just about to *tear it up* when she heard Bobby say "Don't *rip it up*. Keep it. I know what it means to you but someday Lucille might want it because he was her real father."

"You want me to keep it although we are going to be married soon." Molly asked surprisingly.

"Yes. *When a man loves a woman,* then he shares the good times and the bad with her. You were once a *woman in love* with him but he was taken from you so you have spent your life alone with your daughter who didn't even get to meet or know him. I am honored that she would like me to be her father but one day when she is getting married or has children of her own, she may want to know a bit more about him.

If she has any children they may have some of his characteristics and you will be able to answer questions if she has any and you will be able to give her the letter to read if she hasn't already read it." said Bobby tenderly.

Molly looked at him with tears in her eyes and softly said "You will *stand by me* through anything, won't you? You are a *dream lover* and *I'll never find another you* and I will never go looking for one either."

Bobby took her in his arms and said "*It's all right baby.* Come on; you know that *big girls don't cry.*" Then to make her smile he said "*Lover please,* tell me where else will I get *kisses sweeter than wine?*"

Jane made the dresses and added a small blue *sapphire* set in a *band of gold* to Molly's hair band that held her veil on her head.

On their wedding day, *Mr Blue* was running around trying to get everything in order. There were *so many ways* to set everything up but it took him quite a few attempts before he was happy with the final outcome. It looked like there was *sixteen tons* of food and a big mess everywhere.

"*Susie darlin'* don't worry about cleaning that up now, *Sadie the cleaning lady* has just pulled up so she'll do it.

Jeannie, Jeannie, Jeannie; don't put those there. The *roses are red my love* so they should be over by the *mission bell* that is hanging below *the moon of love.*

Come on, *work with me Annie.* Be careful that there's *nothin' shakin'* on those trestles that could fall off and hurt someone.

Mercy. Sorry. Marcy, *Sadie the cleaning lady* will clean over by the stage first so that you can set up the music. I hope that you left your pooch *Ya Ya* at home because he does nothing but howl when you play *Miss You Nights* and then he'll want you to play *I'm a Tiger* for his encore.

Oh Carol, are you ready to start serving drinks when the guests start arriving?" said Mr Blue.

"Yes. *I'm ready.*" replied Carol.

69

Mr. Blue was still flitting around making sure that everything was how he intended it to be when he looked at his watch and called out softly "Places everybody. The bride and groom will be here in *5 – 4 – 3 – 2 – 1*. Let us make it *wonderful tonight* for them. Let's hope that it will be *some enchanted evening* that they will never forget."

During the reception Bobby said affectionately to Molly "Now we are *up where we belong* and *you belong to me* finally. This is *the real thing* for me and I now know the answer to *"Why do fools fall in love?"*

The answer is that they are not fools at the time. The day that I saw you in the chapel is the day I wanted to make you *my girl* but I was afraid that I would only get a *one way* love relationship in return; like I have had so many times before. Today you have become my wife and it's *the wonder of you* and your *personality* that has shown me the *true love ways* to happiness. *The night has a thousand eyes* so they can be a witness to our first night of married life together under both a *blue moon* and a *blue star*. Please *save the last dance for me* and I hope that it will be the *last waltz* of the evening."

He then turned to Lucille and said "*She wears my ring* and I love her, or rather the both of you *more than I can say*."

Molly whispered in his ear "*Lover please* these *are magic moments* for me and *memories are made of this* and other times like these. You also know that the *little things mean a lot* to me and *I'm a believer* in *what ever will be will be*."

Charlie was walking past *Lana* who said to some other girls "*Let's have another party* for Lucille over at my place next month for her birthday. We can invite *Donna* and *Diana* and Mr *Perfect Love* and my mother will agree if we keep it to just a few friends."

"Do you mean Brian? *He's so fine* and when he walks, it's like watching *poetry in motion* walking by. He can be *my babe* and *come softly to me* anytime." asked one of the other girls.

"*Gee whiz*." said a third girl "If you think that he is just *poetry in motion;* then you should look closer, because he is a sonnet. I think it's a great idea for the party but shouldn't we ask Lucille's mother if it all right with her first."

The girls spotted two other friends and called out "*Hello Mary Lou* and *Hey Paula* what are you doing here?"

Charlie couldn't help smiling to himself and thought "*Young love*. They all seemed to be *starry eyed* over one particular boy and in a few months' time they'll be saying the same thing over another boy."

"Lucille, one day you'll be getting married." said Mr Blue.

Lucille looked at him and said "*That'll be the day* when pigs fly and the moon turns blue. There is so much that I want to do and places that I want to go to before I settle down with a *dream lover*.

My life at the moment is just the way *I like it* and if a *teen angel* comes along, I will *tell him* that I'm not interested because I want to study and go to university, if I can get in, even though I don't know what I want to do there yet."

Mr Blue replied "You say that now and in a year or two you'll be saying *long live love* and *love me tender* at your wedding reception. *Over and over* again I hear you young people *rave on* about what you want and what you are going to do and most of the time nothing comes of it. I don't believe that you are any different from the other teenagers and really do what you say you're going to do."

"*Oh; but I do* intend to do what I've said I'm going to do. In the past year I have learnt so much and I have seen so much and I know that whatever I decide to do mom and Bobby will support me and give their *love to me. It's all in the game* of life and I have to play it my way and not somebody else's way if I want to achieve my goals and dreams."

Bobby said "*Love is strange* and can catch you unknowingly. Watch out for the *blue moon* because it can also do *crazy* things to you as well."

Then both he and Molly laughed.

REFERENCE

TRUE FIFTIES ALBUM VARIOUS ARTISTS
DISC I
(We're Gonna) Rock Around The Clock – Bill Haley & His Comets
Sh-Boom - The Crew Cuts
Rock Island Line – Lonnie Donegan
Only You (And You Alone) – The Hilltoppers
I'll Be Home – Pat Boone
The Great Pretender – The Platters
A Sweet Old Fashioned Girl – Teresa Brewer
Giddy Up a Ding Dong – Freddie Bell & The Bellboys
The Green Door – Jim Lowe
Singing The Blues – Tommy Steele and The Steelmen
The Garden Of Eden – Frankie Vaughan
Young Love – Tab Hunter
Little Darlin – The Diamonds
April Love – Pat Boone
A White Sport Coat – Terry Dene
That'll Be The Day – Buddy Holly & The Crickets
Alone – The Southlanders
My Special Angel – Bobby Helms
Sugartime – The McGuire Sisters
DISC 2
Peggy Sue – Buddy Holly
La Dee Dah – Jackie Dennis
Tequila – Ted Heath and his Orchestra
Sweet Little Sixteen – Chuck Berry
The Purple People Eater – Sheb Wooley
Stupid Cupid – Connie Francis
Susie Darlin – Robin Lake
Hoots Mon! – Lord Rockingham's XI
It's Only Make Believe – Conway Twitty
Chantilly Lace – The Big Bopper
Maybe Tomorrow – Billy Fury
Come Softly To Me – Frankie Vaughn & The Kaye Sisters
A Teenager In Love – Marty Wilde
Endlessly – Brook Benton
Personality – Anthony Newley
Sorry (I Ran All The Way Home)
Here Comes Summer – Jerry Keller
Mr Blue – Mike Preston

DISC 3

Auf Wiederseh'n Sweetheart – Vera Lynn
It Takes Two To Tango – Louis Armstrong
Wonderful Copenhagen – Danny Kaye
(How Much Is) That Doggie In The Window – Lita Roza
The Moulin Rouge Theme – Mantovani & His Orchestra
Answer Me – David Whitfield
I See The Moon – The Stargazers
Little Things Mean A Lot – Kitty Kallen
Three Coins In A Fountain – The Four Aces
If I Give My Heart To You – Joan Regan
No One But You – Billy Eckstine
The Finger Of Suspicion – Dickie Valentine
Unchained Melody – Jimmy Young
Blue Star (Medic Theme – Cyril Stapleton
Hernando's Hideaway – The Johnson Brothers
It's Almost Tomorrow – Dream Weavers
Memories Are Made Of This – Dave King
The Poor People Of Paris – Winifred Atwell
Around The World – Bing Crosby

TRUE SIXTIES ALBUM VARIOUS ARTISTS
DISC 1

Hey! Baby – Bruce Channel
Itsy Teeny Weeny Yellow Polka Dot Bikini – Brian Hyland
Handy Man – Jimmy Jones
Robot Man – Connie Francis
Telstar – The Tornados
You're So Square (Baby, I Don't Care) – Buddy Holly
Sweet Nothin's – Brenda Lee
Cradle Of Love – Johnny Preston
Johnny Will – Pat Boone
Became Muncho (Kiss Me) – Jet Harris
Are You Sure? – The Allisons
I'm Just A Baby – Louise Cordet
Runaround Sue – Doug Shelton
Bad Boy – Marty Wilde
Get Lost (In My Arms) – Eden Kane
Lover Please – The Vernons Girls
Entry Of The Gladiators – Nero & The Gladiators
Mysterty Girl – Jess Conrad
Oh! Lonesome Me – Craig Douglas
Island Of Dreams – The Springfields
Wonderous Place – Billy Fury

73

DISC 2

Ain't She Sweet – The Beatles
Twist And Shout – Brian Poole & The Tremeloes
Money – Bera Elliot & The Fenman
Memphis Tennessee – Dave Berry & The Cruisers
Tell Him – Billie Davis
Scarlett O'Hara – Jet Harris & Tony Meehan
My Boy Lollipop – Millie
Tell Me When – The Applejacks
The Clapping Song (Clap Pat Clap Slap) – Shirley Ellis
Um Um Um Um Um Um – Wayne Fontana & The Mindbenders
In The Middle Of Nowhere – Dusty Springfield
Yeh Yeh – Georgie Fame
1, 2, 3 – Len Barry
Wolly Bully – Sam The Sham & The Pharaohs
Pipeline – The Chantays
Sorrow – The Merseys
Semi-Detached Suburban Mr James – Manfred Mann
Sha La La La Lee – Small Faces
Keep On Running – The Spencer Davis Group

DISC 3

Dancing In The Street – Martha Reeves & The Vandellas
I Heard It Through The Grapevine – Marvin Gaye
I Can't Help Myself – Four Tops
Son Of A Preacher Man – Dusty Springfield
Gotta See Jane – R. Dean Taylor
(I'm A) Road Runner – Junior Walker & The All Stars
I'll Pick A Rose For My Rose – Marv Johnson
I'm Gonna Make You Love Me – Diana Ross & The Supremes With The
Temptations
Ain't Nothing Like The Real Thing – Marvin Gaye & Tammi Terrell
Dedicated To The One I Love – The Mamas & The Papas
Paper Sun – Traffic
Wild Thing – The Troggs
Fire-Crazy World of Arthur Brown
Okay! – Dave Dee, Dozy, Beaky, Mick & Tich
Bend Me Shape Me – Amen Corner
Lightnin' Strikes – Lou Christie
Eloise – Barry Ryan
Dizzy – Tommy Roe

LET THE GOOD TIMES ROLL (1960 – 1963)
VARIOUS ARTISIS
DISC 1
Roy Orbison – Dream Baby (How Long Must I Dream)
Lesley Gore – It's My Party
Frank Ifield - I Remember You
Neil Sedaka – Calendar Girl
The Tokens – The Lion Sleeps Tonight
The Drifters – Save The Last Dance For Me
Dion – Runaround Sue
Col Joye – Sweet Little Sixteen Twist
Little Eva – The Locomotion
Ricky Nelson – Hello Mary Lou
Connie Francis – Everybody's Somebody's Fool
Johnny O'Keefe – I'm Counting On You
Clarence "Frogman" Henry – (I Don't Know Why) But I Do
Pat Boone – Moody River
Bobby Vinton – Roses Are Red (My Love)
Ben E King – Stand By Me
Jimmy Little – Royal Telephone
Bobby Vee – Take Good Care Of My Baby
Paul and Paula – Hey Paula
Patsy Cline – Crazy
Ray Peterson – Tell Laura I Love Her
Claude King – Wolverton Mountain
DISC 2
The Beach Boys – Surfin' Safari
The Deltones – Hangin' Five
Brian Hyland – Itsy Bitsy Teeny Weeny Yellow Polka Dot Bikini
The Atlantics – Bombora
The Contours – Do You Love Me
Chuck Berry – No Particular Place To Go
Buzz Clifford – Baby Sittin' Boogie
Bobby Darin – Multiplication
Brenda Lee – Sweet Nothin's
John D Loudermilk – Language Of Love
The Marvelettes – Please Mr Postman
Leroy Van Dyke – Walk On By
Johnny Preston – Cradle Of Love
Clyde McPhatter – Love Please
Dickey Lee – I Saw Linda Yesterday
Ernie K Doe – Mother-In-Law
Tommy Roe – Sheila

Damita Jo – Dance With Dolly
Dave Rose Orchestra – The Stripper
Fats Domino – Jambalaya (On The Bayou)
Duane Eddy – (Dance With The) Guitar Man
Lucky Starr – I've Been Everywhere

SENSATIONAL SIXTIES (2 CD SET)
VARIOUS ARTISTS
DISC 1

Love Grows (Where My Rosemary Goes) – Edison Lighthouse
With A Girl Like You – The Troggs
Lightning Strikes – Lou Christie
Build Me Up Buttercup – The Foundations
How Do You Do It? – Gerry and the Pacemakers
Love On A Mountain Top – Robert Knight
Little Arrows – Leapy Lee
Yellow River – Christie
She's Not There – The Zombies
Dizzy – Tommy Roe
Happy Together – The Turtles
It's My Party – Lesley Gore
Da Doo Ron Ron – The Crystals
Gimme Little Sign – Brenton Wood
The Letter – Box Tops
You've Got Your Troubles – The Fortunes
A Groovy Kind Of Love – Wayne Fontana
Young Girl – Gary Puckett and the Union Gap

DISC 2

Ob La Di Ob La Da – Marmalade
I'm Gonna Make You Mine – Lou Christie
Here It Comes Again – The Fortunes
Tobacco Road – Nashville Teens
Any Way That You Want Me – The Troggs
I'm Telling You Now – Freddie and The Dreamers
I Like It – Gerry and the Pacemakers
Elenore – The Turtles
Baby, Now That I Found You – The Foundations
Baby Come Back – The Equals
Knock On Wood – Eddie Floyd
Soul Man – Sam and Dave
The In Crowd – Dobie Gray
Rescue Me – Fontella Bass
Tighten Up – Archie Bell and the Drells
Then He Kissed Me – The Crystals

Sorrow – The Merseys
Little Children – Billy J Kramer

101 ROCK 'N' ROLL CLASSICS (4 CD BOX SET)
VARIOUS ARTISTS
DISC 1 ROCK ON
Runaway – Del Shannon
Blue Moon – Marcels
The Great Pretender – The Platters
Rubber Ball – Bobby Vee
Baby Face – Little Richard
Wild One – Bobby Rydell
Because They're Young – Duane Eddy
Speedy Gonzalas – Pat Boone
Singing The Blues – Guy Mitchell
Tiger – Fabian
Endlessly – Brook Benton
Along came Jones – The Coasters
Venus – Frankie Avalon
Poetry In Motion – Johnny Tillotson
Devil Or Angel – Bobby Vee
Corina, Corina – Ray Peterson
Beatnik Fly – Johnny And The Hurricanes
Hats Off To Larry – Del Shannon
Let's Have A Party – Wanda Jackson
Venus In Blue Jeans – Jimmy Clanton
Hawaii Five-O – The Ventures
Swingin' School – Bobby Rydell
Let's Go – The Routers
Hey Baby – Bruce Channel
Endless Sleep – Jody Reynolds
DISC 2 JUMPIN' JUKEBOX
Lucille – Little Richard
Yakety Yak – The Coasters
Rockin' Robin – Bobby Day
Teen Beat – Sandy Nelson
Come Go With Me – The Del Vikings
Purple People Eater – Sheb Wooley
Little Darlin' – The Diamonds
Mr Lee – The Bobbettes
Love Potion No 9 – The Clovers
Alley Oop – Hollywood Argyles
Down The Line – Jerry Lee Lewis
The Happy Organ – Dave "Baby" Cortez

Hula Love – Buddy Knox
Ain't That A Shame – Pat Boone
Stagger Lee – Lloyd Price
Red River Rock – Johnny And The Hurricanes
Rebel Rouser – Duane Eddy
Good Golly Miss Molly – Little Richard
Bongo Rock – Preston Epps
Western Movies – The Olympics
Dixie Fried – Carl Perkins
Finger Poppin' Time – Hank Ballard And The Midnighters
Razzle Dazzle (live) – Bill Haley & His Comets
Seven Little Girls (Sitting In The Back Seat) – Paul Evans
Charlie Brown – The Coasters

DISC 3 LOVER'S ROCK

A Rockin' Good Way (To Mess Around and Fall In Love) – Brook Benton
This Magic Moment – The Drifters
Love Letters In The Sand – Pat Boone
Come Softly To Me – The Fleetwoods
Smoke Gets In Your Eyes – The Platters
Sea Of Love – Phil Phillips
Sleep Walk – Santo And Johnny
For Your Precious Love – The Impressions
You Always Hurt The One You Love – Clarence "Frogman" Henry
Susie Darlin' – Robin Luke
Earth Angel – Crew Cuts
I'll Make It Up To You – Jerry Lee Lewis
My Special Angel – Bobby Helms
Primrose Lane – Jerry Wallace
Tell Laura I Love Her – Ray Peterson
Teen Angel – Mark Dinning
What In The World's Come Over You – Jack Scott
Will You Love Me Tomorrow – The Shirelles
He Will Break Your Heart – Jerry Butler
Lavender Blue – Sammy Turner
Hey Little Girl – Dee Clark
My Heart Is An Open Book – Carl Dobkins Jr
Mr Blue – The Fleetwoods
Why? – Frankie Avalon
Lonely Street – Gene Vincent
Only You (And You Alone) – The Platters

DISC 4 JIVE TIME

Walk – Don't Run – The Ventures

78

Do You Wanna Dance – Bobby Freeman
Willie And The Hand Jive – Johnny Otis
Let's Go, Let's Go, Let's Go – Hank Ballard And The Midnighters
Forty Miles Of Bad Road – Duane Eddy
Let There Be Drums – Sandy Nelson
A Wonderful Time Up There – Pat Boone
Sorry (I Ran All The Way Home) – The Impalas
Keep A Knockin' – Little Richard
Rock 'n' Roll Is Here To Stay – Danny And The Juniors
Reville Rock – Johnny And The Hurricanes
Ooby Dooby – Roy Orbison
Blue Suede Shoes – Carl Perkins
At The Hop – Danny And The Juniors
Honky Tonk (Part 2) – Bill Dogget
Personality – Lloyd Price
Little Bitty Pretty One – Bobby Day
Jenny Jenny – Little Richard
This Ole House – Rosemary Clooney
The Green Door – Jim Lowe
Party Doll – Buddy Knox
Searchin' – The Coasters
Raunchy – Bill Justis
Tutti Frutti – Little Richard
Rock Around The Clokck (live) – Bill Haley And His Comets

101 TRACKS OF UNFORGETABLE LOVE (4 CD BOX SET)
VARIOUS ARTISTS
DISC 1 HALFWAY TO PARADISE
Save The Last Dance For Me – The Drifters
More Than I Can Say – The Chiffons
Sweet Talkin' Guy – The Chiffons
Halfway To Paradise – Billy Fury
Dedicated To The One I Love – The Shirelles
It Keeps Right On A Hurtin' Johnny Tillotson
So Much In Love – The Tymes
My Guy – Mary Wells
Can't Take My Eyes Off You – Jay Black, formerly of Jay & The
Americans
Remember Your Mine – Pat Boone
Come Softly To Me – Fleetwoods
In The Misty Moonlight – Jerry Wallace
Mountain Of Love – Harold Dorman
(I Don't Know Why) But I Do – Clarence "Frogman" Henry
How Sweet It Is (To Be Loved By You) – Sam & Dave

79

For Your Precious Love – The Impressions
You Belong To Me – The Duprees
Then You Can Tell Me Goodbye – The Casinos
I Say A Little Prayer – Martha Reeves
Endlessly – Brook Benton
Let It Be Me – Betty Everett & Jerry Butler
Gee Whiz (Look At his Eyes) – Carla Thomas
Earth Angel (Will You Be Mine) - The Penguines
The Great Pretender – The Platters
You Send Me – Percy Sledge

DISC 2 LOVE ON THE ROCK

I've Been Loving You Too Long – Percy Sledge
He's Out Of My Life – Gloria Gaynor
Unchained Melody – The Drifters
What Kind Of Fool (Do You Think I Am) – The Tams
You've Lost That Loving Feeling – Timi Yuro
Lovin' Arms – Dobie Gray
Goin' Out Of My Head – Little Anthony & The Imperials
Since I Don't Have You – The Skyliners
You'll Lose a Good Thing – Barbara Lynn
If You Don't Know Me By Now – Harold Melvin & The Bluenotes
Two Lovers – Mary Wells
What Becomes Of The Broken Hearted? – Jimmy Ruffin
Help Me Make It Through The Night – Sammi Smith
I Will – Ruby Winters
Tell It Like It Is – Aaron Neville
I (Who Have Nothing) Ben E King
Smoke Gets In Your Eyes – The Platters
Will You Love Me Tomorrow – The Shirelles
It's Just A Matter Of Time – Brook Benton
All I Could Do Was Cry – Etta James
I Know (You Don't Love Me No More) – Barbara George
Take Good Care Of Her – Adam Wade
Raindrops – Dee Clark
You Always Hurt The One You Love – Clarence "Frogman" Henry
He Will Break Your Heart – Jerry Butler
Sea Of Love – Phil Phillips

DISC 3 LAUGHTER & TEARS

Somewhere – P J Proby
It's Only Make Believe – Bill Fury
Close To You – B J Thomas
Up Where We Belong – Ace Cannon
Solitaire – Glenn Yarborough

Little Things Mean A Lot – Timi Yuro
Red Roses For A Blue Lady – Vic Dana
I'll Be Home – Pat Boone
Just Walkin' In The Rain – Jonnie Ray
Band Of Gold – Mel Carter
Love Is A Golden Ring – Frankie Laine
Autumn Leaves – Roger Williams
You Don't Have To Say You Love Me – Lynn Anderson
Love Is All Around – The Troggs
The Crying Game – Dave Berry
Crying – Jay Black, formerly of Jay & The Americans
I Love How You Love Me – Sandy Posey
For the Good Times – Ray Price
Forget Him – Bobby Rydell
My Heart Is An Open Book – Carl Dobkins Jr
I Can't Stop Loving You – Don Gibson
The End Of The World – Skeeter Davis
Rhythm Of The Rain – The Cascades
Mr Blue – The Fleetwoods
Deep Purple – Nino Tempo & April Stevens
DISC 4 LOVE DREAMS
Cupid – The Drifters
Every Time You Go Away – Gloria Gaynor
Stand By Me – Ben E King
Raindrops Keep Fallin' On My Head – B J Thomas
I'd Love You To want me – Lobo
Looking For Love – Johnny Lee
Only Love Can Break A Heart – Timi Yuro
So Many Ways – Brook Benton
Just One Look – Doris Troy
Hey There Lonely Girl – Eddie Holman
The Impossible Dream – Roger Williams
Moon River – Jerry Butler
Only You (And You Alone) – The Platters
When A Man Loves A Woman – Percy Sledge
Baby It's You – The Shirelles
You Keep Me Hangin' On – Joe Simon
I Love The Way You Love Me – Marv Johnson
Wonderful! Wonderful! – The Tymes
Hold Me, Thrill Me, Kiss Me – Mel Carter
Chapel Of Love – The Dixie Cups
Lavender Blue – Sammy Turner
My Own True Love – The Duprees

81

The Long And Winding Road – Ace Cannon
Too Weak To Fight – Clarence Carter
Something's Got A Hold On Me – Etta James

K O ROCKERS ROCK-N-ROLL
50 NON STOP HITS
VARIOUS ARTISTS (NO NAMES GIVEN ON COVER)
Rock On Rock "N' Roll
Rock Around The Clock
Good Golly Miss Molly
Memphis Tennessee
Sweet Little Sixteen
Roll Over Beethoven
Bye Bye Johnny
Rock And Roll Music
Peggy Sue
Brown-Eyed Handsome Man
Oh Boy
C'mon Everybody
Summertime Blues
Marie Marie
The Hucklebuck
Be-Bop-A-Lula
Hound Dog
Jailhouse Rock
Rip It Up
All Shook Up
Blue Suede Shoes
Long Tall Sally
At The Hop
Let's Have A party
Rock On Rock 'N' Roll
My Girl Josephine
I'm Ready
Baby Face
Whole Lot Of Shakin
High School
Confidential
Great balls Of Fire
Runaway
Wipe Out
Red River '81
Rock 'N' Roll is Still Alive
Ready Teddy

82

Runaround Sue
In New Orleans
The Girl Can't Help It
Chantilly Lace
Kansas City
I Need Your Love Tonight
Poison Ivy
Apron Strings
Palisades Park
Rock Me Baby
Yakaty Yak
Give Me Love
Rock On Rock 'N' Roll

MEMORIES ARE MADE OF THIS
VARIOUS ARTISTS
DISC ONE
Memories Are Made Of This
What Ever Will Be Will Be
Perry Como - Magic Moments
Neil Sedaka – Diana
Connie Francis – Lipstick On Your Collar
Bobby Darrin – Dream Lover
Buddy Holly – Heartbeat
Everley Brothers – All I Have To Do Is Dream
Frankie Avalon – Venus
The Fleetwoods – Come Softly To Me
Connie Stevens – Sixteen Reasons
Johnny Ray – Just Walkin' In The Rain
Guy Mitchell – Singing The Blues
Buddy Knox – Party Doll
Adam Faith – What Do You Want
Sonny James – Young Love
Stonewall Jackson – Waterloo
Marty Robbins – The Story Of My Life
Jimmie Rodgers – Kisses Sweeter Than Wine
The Four Preps – Big Man
Slim Whitman – Rose Marie
Vic Damone – On The Street Where You Live
Tennessee Ernie Ford – Sixteen Tons
Frankie Laine – I Believe
Jo Stafford – You Belong To Me
Harry Belafonte – Jamaica Farewell
Debbie Reynolds –Tammy

The Platters – Smoke Gets In Your Eyes
Rosemary Clooney - Hey There
Andy Williams – Hawaiian Wedding Song
Ritchie Valens – Donna
The Flamingos – I Only Have Eyes For You
DISC TWO
Roy Orbison – Only The Lonely
The Shirelles – Will You Love Me Tomorrow
Neil Sedaka – Calendar Girl
Johnny Tillotson – Poetry In Motion
Clarence "Frogman" Henry – (I Don't Know Why) But I Do
Jimmy Jones – Good Timin'
Gene McDonald – Tower Of Strength
Bobby Vee – Rubber Ball
Dion – Runaround Sue
The Drifters – Save The Last Dance For Me
Carole King – It Might As Well Rain Until September
Donnie Brooks – Doll House
Craig Douglas – Time
Marv Johnson – You Got What It Takes
Johnny Burnette – You're Sixteen
Emile Ford & The Checkmates – What Do You Want To Make Those
Eyes At Me For?
Del Shannon – Runaway
The Cascades – Rhythm Of The Rain
Joe Jones – You Talk Too Much
The Marcels – Blue moon
Frank Ifield – I Remember You
Brian Hyland – Sealed with A Kiss
Ray Peterson – Tell Laura I Love Her
Nat King Cole – Ramblin' Rose
Jim Reeves – He'll Have To Go
Jeanne Black – He'll Have To Stay
Bobby Vinton – Blue Velvet
Al Martino – I Love You Because
Shirley Bassey – As Long As He Needs Me
Danny Williams – Moon River
Petula Clark – Sailor
Ray Coniff & The Singers – Somewhere My Love
DISC THREE
Cliff Richard & The Shadows – The Young Ones
Dusty Springfield – I Only Want To Be With You
Trini Lopez – If I Had A Hammer

Gene Pitney – The Man Who Shot Liberty Valance
Helen Shapiro – Walkin' Back To Happiness
Lesley Gore – It's My Party
Tom Jones – Help Yourself
Sandie Shaw – (There's) Always Something There To Remind Me
P J Proby – Mission Bell
Vikki Carr – It Must Be Him
Glen Campbell – By The Time I Get To Phoenix
Matt Monro – Born Free
Lulu – To Sir With Love
Billy J Kramer & The Dakotas – Trains And Boats And Planes
Solomon King – She Wears My Ring
Ken Dodd – Tears
Cilla Black – You're My World (Il Mio Mondo)
B J Thomas – Mama
The Shangri-Las – The Leader Of The Pack
The Essex – Easier Said Than done
The Bachelors – Diane
Bobby Goldsboro – Honey
The Seekers – I'll Never Find Another You
John Rowles – If I Only Had Time
Engelbert Humperdinck – The Last Waltz
Gerry & The Pacemakers – You'll Never Walk Alone
Elvis Presley – Can't Help Falling In Love

COMPLETE SIXTIES
VARIOUS ARTISTS
DISC 1: 1960 – 1961
Marv Johnson – You Got What It Takes
Johnny Ashcroft – Little Boy Lost
Rolf Harris – Tie Me Kangaroo Down Mate
Jeanne Black – He'll Have To Stay
Wanda Jackson – Let's Have A Party
The Pittdown Men – Brontosaurus Stomp
Johnny Burnett – You're Sixteen
Joe Jones – You Talk Too Much
The Ventures – Perfidia
Peter Sellers & Sophia Loren – Goodness Gracious Me
Edith Piaf – Milord
Bobby Vee – Rubber Ball
Ferlin Husky – Wings Of A dove
Don Costa, His Orchestra & Chorus – Never On Sunday
Ferrante & Teicher – Exodus (Theme From Otto Preminger's "Exodus")
The Marcels – Blue Moon

Andy Stewart – A Scottish Soldier
Gene McDaniels – A Hundred Pounds Of Clay
Ernie K-Doe – Mother-in -Law
Bryan Davies – Dream Girl
DISC 2: 1961 – 1963
Craig Douglas – Time
James Darren – Goodbye Cruel World
Charlie Drake – My Boomerang Won't Come Back
Sandy Nelson – Let There Be Drums
Joey Dee & The Starlighters – Peppermint Twist
Dion – The Wanderer
Walter Brennan With The Johnny Mann Singers – Old Rivers
Frank Ifield – I Remember You
Little Eva – The Locomotion
Ned Miller – From A Jack To A King
The Shadows – The Boys
The Denvermen – Surfside
The Exciters – Tell Him
Jay Justin – Proud Of You
Kyu Sakamoto – Sukiyaki
Jan & Dean – Surf City
Wayne Newton – Danke Schoen
Al Martino – Painted Tainted Rose
Helen Shapiro – Not Responsible
Gerry & The Pacemakers – You'll Never Walk Alone
DISC 3: 1963 – 1965
Little Pattie – He's My Blonde Headed, Stompie Wompie Real Gone
Surfer Boy
Jody Miller – He Walks Like A Man
The Swinging Blue Jeans – Hippy Hippy Shake
Billy J Kramer & The Dakotas – Little Children
Cilla Black – You're My World (Il Mio Mondo)
The Animals – The House Of The Rising Sun
Manfred Mann – Do Wah Diddy Diddy
The Nashville Teens – Tobacco Road
Sounds Incorporated – William Tell Overture
Jay & The Americans – Come A Little Bit Closer
The Seekers – I'll Never Find Another You
Gary Lewis & The Playboys – This Diamond Ring
Adam Faith – It's Alright
Shirley Bassey – Goldfinger
Herman's Hermits – Mrs Brown You've Got A Lovely Daughter
P J Proby Mission Bell

Brendan Bowyer – The Hucklebuck
The Sunrays – I Live For The Sun
The Toys – A Lover's Concerto
Ken Dodd – Tears
DISC 4: 1965 – 1967
The Fourmost – Girls, Girls, Girls
Cher – Bang Bang (My Baby Shot Me Down)
Grantley Dee – Let The Little Girl Dance
Verdelle Smith – Tar And Cement
Matt Monro – Born Free
The Hollies – Bus Stop
The Twilights – Needle In A Haystack
Peter & Gordon – Lady Godiva
Cliff Bennett & The Rebel Rousers – Got To Get You Int6o My Life
The Beach Boys – Good Vibrations
Bev Harrell – What Am I Doing Here With You
Paul Jones – I've Been A Bad Bad Boy
The Vibrants – Something About You, Baby
Cheryl Gray – You Made Me What I Am
Jeff Beck – Hi Ho Silver Lining
Vikki Carr – It Must Be Him (Seul Sur Son Etoile)
Bobbie Gentry – Ode To Billy Joe
Lulu – To Sir With Love
Johnny Farnham – Sadie, The Cleaning Lady
The Stone Ponies featuring Linda Ronstadt – Different Drum
DISC 5: 1967 – 1969
The Groove – Soothe Me
Solomon King – She Wears My Ring
Bobby Goldsboro – Honey
Canned Heat – On The Road Again
The Band – The Weight
Deep Purple – Kentucky Woman
New World – Try To Remember
The Scaffold – Lily The Pink
The Bonzo Dog Doo Dah Band – I'm The Urban Spaceman
Tommy James & The Shondells – Crimson And Clover
Joe South – The Games People Play
Peter Sarstedt – Where Do You Go To (My Lovely)
Russell Morris – The Real Thing
Glen Campbell – Galveston
The Flying Circus – La La
Oliver – Good Morning Starshine
Jackie De Shannon – Put A Little Love In Your Heart

Doug Parkinson In Focus – Without You
Axiom – Arkansas Grass
Masters Apprentices – Think About Tomorrow Today

BEST OF ROCK 'N' ROLL - GREATEST ORIGINALS FROM THE 50S & 60S VARIOUS ARTISTS

Oh Carol - Neil Sedaka
Sweet Nothings - Brenda Lee
Only the Lonely - Roy Orbison
Kiss Me Quick - Elvis Presley
Hello Mary Lou - Ricky Nelson
Runaround Sue - Dion
Don't Be Cruel - Elvis Presley
Say Mama - Gene Vincent
Diana - Paul Anka
Corinna, Corinna - Ray Peterson
Runaway - Del Shannon
Walking Back to Happiness - Helen Shapiro
Raunchy - Bill Justis
Breathless - Jerry Lee Lewis
Calendar Girl - Neil Sedaka
I Love You Baby - Paul Anka
Don't Knock the Rock - Bill Haley & His Comets
Somke Gets in Your Eyes - The Platters
Hello Josephine - Fats Domino
Keep a Knockin' - Little Richard
Come Go With Me - The Del Vikings
Three Steps to Heaven - Eddie Cochran
Love Letters in the Sand - Pat Boone
Ginger Bread - Frankie Avalon
The Lion Sleeps - Tonight The Tokens
Little Darlin' - The Diamonds
Stay - Maurice Williams & The Zodiacs
Chi Chi - John Buck & His Blazers
Sugartime - The Mc Guire Sisters
Stupid Cupid - Wanda Jackson
Singing the Blues - Guy Mitchell
Ya Ya - Lee Dorsey
Race With the Devil - Gene Vincent & His Blue Caps
It's Now or Never - Elvis Presley
Hit the Road Jack - Ray Charles
Problems - The Everly Brothers
I'll Be Home - Pat Boone
Susie Darlin' - Robin Luke

All I Have to Do Is Dream - The Everly Brothers
I'm Walking - Fats Domino
Tweedlee Dee - Frankie Vaughn
Little Bitty Pretty One - Clyde Mc Phatter
At My Front Door - The El Dorados

ROCK 'N' ROLL HIT COLLECTION FROM 50's & 60's
VARIOUS ARTISTS

Nothin' Shakin' - (but the Leaves On the Trees) Eddie Fontaine
Move It - Cliff Richard
Up Above My Head I Hear Music in the Air - Laurie London
Jailhouse Rock - Elvis Presley
There's Good Rockin' Tonight - Ricky Nelson
Please Mr. Mayor - Roy Clark
You Got Me Reeling and Rocking - Roy Milton
Gee - The Crows
Shirley - Lee Ricky Nelson
Yakety Yak - The Coasters
Mean Woman Blues - Jerry Lee Lewis
Jeannie, Jeannie, Jeannie - Eddie Cochran
Sincerely - The Moonglows
Lucille - Little Richard
Hound Dog - Elvis Presley
Shortnin' Bread - Paul Chaplain & His Emeralds
Long Gone Daddy - Pat Cupp
You Cash Ain't Nothin' but Trash - The Clovers
Lipstick, Powder and Paint - Big Joe Turner
All Right Baby - Janis Martin
Itchy Twitchy Feeling - Bobby Hendricks
Six-Five Jive - Jimmy Jackson
Rock 'n' Roll Deacon - Screamin' Joe Neal
Dizzy Miss Lizzy - Larry Williams
Stranded in the Jungle - The Cadets
Book of Love - The Monotones
Flying Saucer Rock 'n' Roll - Billy Riley
Crawfishin' - Clarence Garlow
Not Fade Away - Buddy Holly
Slow Down - Larry Williams
Shake Baby Shake - Jesse Lee Turner
Rock-A-Billy Boogie - John Barry Seven
Lorraine - Buddy Covelle
I'm in Love Again - Fats Domino
Mercy - The Collins Kids
Mr. Lee - The Bobbettes

Flip Out - Billy Brown
Baby Let's Play House - Elvis Presley
Susie Q - Dale Hawkins
Ooby Dooby - Roy Orbison
Zing Went the Strings of My Heart - The Dallas Boys
Rockin' the Joint - Esquerita
Bad Motorcycle - The Vernon Girls
Oh Little Girl - Dee Clark
Sapphire - Big Danny Oliver
Lovin' Machine - Wynonie Harris
Come Back, Maybellene - Mercy Dee
High Class Baby - Cliff Richard
Ain't Got No Home - Clarence "Frogman" Henry
Fast Freight - Arvee Allens
Evenin' Time - Scotty Mc Kay
Rock On - Buddy Johnson & His Orchestra
Jump, Jive, An' Wail - Louis Prima
Tallahassee Lassie - Freddie Cannon
Ready Teddy - Little Richard
Tear Drops - Lee Andrews & The Hearts
Big Green Car - Billy Carroll
Chicken Shack Boogie - Amos Milburn
Real Wild Child - Ivan
Look Out Mabel - G. L. Crockett
Bip Bop Bip - Pretty Boy
That's All Right - Elvis Presley
I'll Always Be in Love With You - Fats Domino
There Goes My Baby - The Drifters
Roll, Hot Rod, Roll - Oscar Mc Lollie
Well I'm Your Man - Johnny Tillotson
Hit, Git and Split - Young Jessie
I Like Love - Roy Orbison
Why - The Cues
Only You - The Platters
Seventeen - Boyd Bennett & His Rockets
I'll Come Running Back to You - Sam Cooke
Rockin' Robin - Bobby Day
Hey, Hey, Hey, Hey - Cuddly Dudley
Little Miss Ruby - Neville Taylor & The Cutters
Try Me - Bob Luman
Believe What You - Say Ricky Nelson

100 GREATEST HITS OF ROCK 'N' ROLL VARIOUS ARTISTS

Runaround Sue Dion
The Lion Sleeps Tonight The Tokens
Hit the Road Jack Ray Charles
Runaway Del Shannon
Come Go With Me The Del Vikings
Little Darlin' The Diamonds
Stay Maurice Williams & The Zodiacs
All I Have to do Is Dream The Everly Brothers
Little Bitty Pretty One Clyde Mc Phatter
Somke Gets in Your Eyes The Platters
Corinna, Corinna Ray Peterson
Only the Lonely Roy Orbison
Oh Carol Neil Sedaka
Sweet Nothings Brenda Lee
Hello Mary Lou Ricky Nelson
Diana Paul Anka
Walking Back to Happiness Helen Shapiro
Raunchy Bill Justis
Breathless Jerry Lee Lewis
Don't Knock the Rock Bill Haley & His Comets
Hello Josephine Fats Domino
Keep a Knockin' Little Richard
Three Steps to Heaven Eddie Cochran
Love Letters in the Sand Pat Boone
Ginger Bread Frankie Avalon
Chi Chi John Buck & His Blazers
Sugartime The Mc Guire Sisters
Stupid Cupid Wanda Jackson
Singing the Blues Guy Mitchell
Ya Ya Lee Dorsey
Race With the Devil Gene Vincent & His Blue Caps
Susie Darlin' Robin Luke
Tweedlee Dee Frankie Vaughn
At My Front Door The El Dorados
Long Tall Sally Little Richard
Don't Ha Ha Huey Piano Smith
Vacation Connie Francis
My Gal Is Red Hot Billy Lee Riley
Over and Over Bobby Day
La Bamba Ritchie Valens
I Wonder Why Dion & The Belmonts
Roll Over Beethoven Chuck Berry

Ballad of a Teenage Queen Johnny Cash
Rockin' Pneumonia and the Boogie Huey Piano Smith
Raunchy Ernie Freeman
My Babe Dale Hawkins
Blue Suede Shoes Carl Perkins
Little Bitty Pretty One Frankie Lymon
Tequila The Champs
Hula Hop The Platters
Lollipop The Chordettes
A Wonderful Time Up There Pat Boone
Rock-A-Billy Guy Mitchell
In the Mood Glenn Miller
That'll Be the Day Buddy Holly
Chantilly Lace Big Bopper
Reet Petite Jackie Wilson
Come On Let's Go Ritchie Valens
Party Doll Buddy Knox
Raunchy Ernie Freeman
Over and Over Bobby Day
Summertime Blues Eddie Cochran
Honeycomb Jimmy Rodgers
Race With the Devil Gene Vincent & His Blue Caps
Do You Want to Dance Bobby Freeman
Great Balls of Fire Jerry Lee Lewis
Brand New Cadillac Vince Taylor & The Playboys
Blue Moon The Marcels
Stay Maurice Williams & The Zodiacs
Poetry in Motion Johnny Tillotson
Chi Chi John Buck & His Blazers
Stand By Me Ben E. King
Ya Ya Lee Dorsey
Apache The Shadows
Calendar Girl Neil Sedaka
Itsy Bitsy Teenie Weenie Yellow Polkadot Bikini Bryan Hyland
The Lion Sleeps Tonight The Tokens
Runaround Sue Dion
Save the Last Dance for Me The Drifters
Hello Mary Lou Ricky Nelson
Susie Darlin' Robin Luke
Diana Paul Anka
Oh Lonesome Me Don Gibson
Sugartime The Mc Guire Sisters
Love Letters in the Sand Pat Boone

Singing the Blues Guy Mitchell
Tweedlee Dee Frankie Vaughn
Sweet Nothings Brenda Lee
Raunchy Bill Justis
Don't Ha Ha Huey Piano Smith
Little Bitty Pretty One Frankie Lymon
White Christmas Bing Crosby
Let it Snow, Let it Snow, Let it Snow Frank Sinatra
Silver Bells Dean Martin
Christmastime All Over the World Sammy Davis, Jr.
Merry Christmas The Cameos
Have Yourself a Merry Little Christmas Rosemary Clooney
It's Christmas Time Again Peggy Lee
Christmas Alphabet Dickie Valentine

VARIOUS? – ROCK N' ROLL HITS 50s & 60s 3 × CD, COMPILATION
1-1–Frankie Avalon – Venus
1-2- –Fabian - Turn Me Loose
1-3 - –Dee Clark Hey Little Girl
1-4 - –Jody Reynolds -Endless Sleep
1-5 - -–Miss Toni Fisher* The Big Hurt
1-6 –Billy & Lillie- La Dee Dah
1-7 –Cathy Carr -Ivory Tower
1-8 –Dicky Doo & The Don'ts -Click Clack
1-9-–Jan & Dean -Baby Talk
1-10 -–Santo & Johnny -Tear Drop
2-1 -–Frankie Avalon -DeDe Dinah
2-2 –Fabian -Tiger
2-3 –Olympics, The -Western Movies
2-4 -–Dicky Doo & The Don'ts- Nee Nee Na Na Na Na Nu Nu
2-5 –Dorsey Burnette -(There Was A) Tall Oak Tree
2-6 –Donnie Brooks -Mission Bell
2-7 –Frankie Avalon -Bobby Sox To Stockings
2-8 –Cathy Jean & Roommates, The -Please Love Me Forever
2-9 –Fendermen, The -Mule Skinner Blues
2-10 –Harold Dorman -Mountain Of Love
3-1 –Gene Chandler -Duke Of Earl
3-2 –Frankie Avalon -Why
3-3 –Fabian -Hound Dog Man
3-4 –Larry Verne -Mr. Custer
3-5 –Hollywood Argyles -Alley Oop
3-6 –Paradons, The -Diamonds And Pearls
3-7 –Lee Dorsey -Ya Ya

3-8 –Lonnie Mack -Memphis
3-9 –Moments, The -Walk Right In
3-10 –Paul & Paula -Hey Paula

VARIOUS?– BABY LOVE - 100 CLASSIC LOVE SONGS
OF THE 50's And 60's
4 × CD, COMPILATION BOX SET
1-1 –Supremes, The -Baby Love
1-2 –Elvis Presley -It's Now Or Never
1-3 –Bobby Vee -The Night Has A Thousand Eyes
1-4 –Jackie Wilson -Lonely Teardrops
1-5 –Paul & Paula -Hey Paula
1-6 –Pat Boone -April Love
1-7 –Dion -Runaround Sue
1-8 –Exciters, The -Tell Him
1-9 –Marcels, The -Blue Moon
1-10 –Tommy Roe -Sheila
1-11 -Perry Como -Magic Moments
1-12 –Chordettes, The -Mr. Sandman
1-13 –Ben E. King - Spanish Harlem
1-14 –Timi Yuro -Hurt
1-15 –Brian Hyland -Sealed With A Kiss
1-16 –Connie Francis -Everybody's Somebody's Fool
1-17 –Shelley Fabares -Johnny Angel
1-18 –Blue Diamonds* -Ramona
1-19 –Chiffons, The -One Fine Day
1-20 –Acker Bilk -Stranger On The Shore
1-21 –Jimmy Clanton -Venus In Blue Jeans
1-22 –Everly Brothers, The* -('Till) I Kissed You
1-23 –Fleetwoods, The -Come Softly To Me
1-24 –Platters, The -My Prayer
1-25 –Sonny James -Young Love
2-1 –Cliff Richard & The Shadows -Theme For A Dream
2-2 –Dixie Cups, The -Chapel Of Love
2-3 –Shangri-Las, The -Leader Of The Pack
2-4 –Vic Dana -Red Roses For A Blue Lady
2-5 –Patsy Cline -Crazy
2-6 –Sam Cooke -Cupid
2-7 –Platters, The -Twillight Time
2-8 –Little Anthony & The Imperials -Tears On My Pillow
2-9 –Essex, The -Easier Said Than Done
2-10 –Bobby Helms -My Special Angels
2-11 –Gene Pitney -If I Didn't Have A Dime
2-12 –Bobby Vee -Take Good Care Of My Baby

2-13 –Shirelles, The -Will You Love Me Tomorrow
2-14 –Frankie Avalon -Venus
2-15 –Billy Vaughn And His Orchestra -Sail Along Silv'ry Moon
2-16 –Roy Orbison -Only The Lonely (Know The Way I Feel)
2-17 –Neil Sedaka -Oh! Carol
2-18 –Dion -The Wanderer
2-19 –Skyliners, The -Since I Don't Have You
2-20 –Lesley Gore -It's My Party
2-21 –Mark Dinning -Teen Angel
2-22 –Johnny Tillotson -Poetry In Motion
2-23 –Brenda Lee -All Alone Am I
2-24 –Conway Twitty -It's Only Make Believe
2-25 –Frankie Laine -Answer Me
3-1 –Pat Boone -Love Letters In The Sand
3-2 –Roy Orbison -Oh Pretty Woman
3-3 –Tommy Edwards -It's All In The Game
3-4 –Henry Mancini -Moon River
3-5 –Del-Vikings, The* -Come Go With Me
3-6 –Shangri-Las, The -Remember
3-7 –Del Shannon -Runaway
3-8 –Neil Sedaka -Calender Girl
3-9 –Lesley Gore -You Don't Own Me
3-10 –Bobby Vinton -Blue Velvet
3-11 –Lloyd Price -Personality
3-12 –Brian Hyland -Itsy Bitsy Teenie Weeny Yellow Polka Dot Bikini
3-13 –Blue Diamonds, The -Little Ship
3-14 –Marvelettes, The -Please Mr Postman
3-15 –Diamonds, The -Little Darlin'
3-16 –Terry Stafford -Suspicion
3-17 –Platters, The -Only You (And You Alone)
3-18 –Connie Francis -Lipstick On Your Collar
3-19 –Gene Pitney -Twenty Four Hours From Tulsa
3-20 –Dion & The Belmonts -A Teenager In Love
3-21 –Frankie Avalon -Why
3-22 –Flamingos, The -I Only Have Eyes For You
3-23 –Supremes, The -Where Did Our Love Go
3-24 –Paul Anka -Dance On Little Girl
3-25 –Dusty Springfield -Wishin' And Hopin'
4-1 –Doris Day -Que Sera, Sera
4-2 –Dinah Washington -What A Diffrence A Day Makes
4-3 –Jim Reeves -He'll Have To Go
4-4 –Del Shannon -Keep Searchin' (We'll Follow The Sun)
4-5 –Al Martino -Spanish Eyes

4-6 –Dusty Springfield -I Only Want To Be With You
4-7 –Brian Hyland -Ginny Come Lately
4-8 –Little Peggy March -I Will Follow Him
4-9 –Perry Como -Catch A Falling Star
4-10 –Skeeter Davis -The End Of The World
4-11 –Bobby Vinton -Roses Are Red (My Love)
4-12 –Jay & The Americans -Come A Little Bit Closer
4-13 –Gene Pitney -Only Love Can Break A Heart
4-14 –Roy Orbison -Lana
4-15 –Bruce Channel -Hey! Baby
4-16 –Johnny Mathis -The Twelfth Of Never
4-17 –Ronettes, The -Be My Baby
4-18 –Brothers Four, The -The Green Leaves Of Summer
4-19 –Ray Peterson -Tell Laura I Love Her
4-20 –Neil Sedaka -Breaking Up Is Hard To Do
4-21 –Cliff Richard & Drifters, The -Living Doll
4-22 –Brenda Lee -I'm Sorry
4-23 –Maurice Williams & The Zodiacs -Stay
4-24 –Paul Anka -Put Your Head On My Shoulder
4-25 –Fats Domino -Blueberry Hill

101 ROCK N ROLL HITS [BOX SET]
Disc: 1
1. Big Joe Turner - Shake, Rattle And Roll
2. Bill Haley & His Comets - (We're Gonna) Rock Around The Clock
3. Chuck Berry - Rock And Roll Music
4. Elvis Presley - Jailhouse Rock
5. Little Richard - Tutti Frutti
6. Danny & The Juniors - At The Hop
7. Jerry Lee Lewis - Whole Lotta Shakin' Goin' On
8. The Crickets - That'll Be The Day
9. The Everly Brothers - Wake Up Little Susie
10. Eddie Cochran - Twenty Flight Rock
11. Carl Perkins - Blue Suede Shoes
12. Sanford Clark - The Fool
13. Warren Smith - Red Cadillac And A Black Moustache
14. Gene Vincent - Be-Bop-A-Lula
15. Buddy Knox - Party Doll
16. Thurston Harris & The Sharps - Little Bitty Pretty One
17. Jackie Wilson - Reet Petite
18. Huey "Piano" Smith & The Clowns - Don't You Just Know It
19. LaVern Baker - Jim Dandy
20. Fats Domino - I'm Walkin'
21. Neil Sedaka - I Go Ape

22. Larry Williams - Bony Moronie
23. Bobby Freeman - Do You Wanna Dance
24. The Clovers - Love Potion No. 9
25. Dion & The Belmonts - A Teenager In Love
26. Shirley & Lee - Let The Good Times Roll
27. The Johnny Otis Show - Willie And The Hand Jive
28. Bill Justis - Raunchy
29. Johnny & The Hurricanes - Red River Rock

Disc: 2

1. Fats Domino - Ain't That A Shame
2. The Everly Brothers - Bird Dog
3. Eddie Cochran - Summertime Blues
4. Jerry Lee Lewis - Great Balls Of Fire
5. Little Richard - Long Tall Sally
6. Gene Vincent & His Blue Caps - Blue Jean Bop
7. Eddie Cochran - C'mon Everybody
8. Larry Williams - Dizzy Miss Lizzy
9. Little Richard - Lucille
10. Jerry Lee Lewis - Breathless
11. Fats Domino - I'm In Love Again
12. Gene Vincent - She She Little Sheila
13. Vince Taylor & The Playboys - Brand New Cadillac
14. Eddie Cochran - Somethin' Else
15. Larry Williams - Short Fat Fannie
16. Gene Vincent - Race With The Devil
17. Huey "Piano" Smith & The Clowns - Rockin' Pneumonia And The Boogie Woogie Flu
18. Ricky Nelson - It's Late
19. Frankie Lymon & The Teenagers - Why Do Fools Fall In Love
20. Fats Domino - Blueberry Hill
21. Little Anthony & The Imperials - Tears On My Pillow
22. The Flamingos - I Only Have Eyes For You (Dames)
23. The Five Satins - In The Still Of The Night

Disc: 3

1. Roy Orbison - Only The Lonely (Know The Way I Feel)
2. Eddie Cochran - Three Steps To Heaven
3. Marv Johnson - You Got What It Takes
4. Ricky Nelson - Hello Mary Lou (Goodbye Heart)
5. Bobby Darin - Dream Lover
6. Johnny Burnette - You\x{2019}re Sixteen
7. Curtis Lee - Pretty Little Angel Eyes
8. Dion - Runaround Sue
9. The Four Seasons - Big Girls Don't Cry

10. Del Shannon - Runaway
11. Bobby Vee - Take Good Care Of My Baby
12. Johnny Tillotson - Poetry In Motion
13. Little Eva - The Locomotion
14. Chris Montez - Let\x{2019}s Dance
15. The Beach Boys - Surfin' U.S.A.
16. Jan & Dean - Surf City
17. Dion - The Wanderer
18. Gene McDaniels - Tower Of Strength
19. Bobby Vee - The Night Has A Thousand Eyes
20. Johnny Burnette - Cincinnati Fireball
21. B. Bumble & The Stingers - Nut Rocker
22. Sandy Nelson - Let There Be Drums
23. Frankie Valli & The Four Seasons - Sherry
24. The Marcels - Blue Moon
25. Maurice Williams & The Zodiacs - Stay
26. The Showmen - It Will Stand
27. Jack Scott feat. The Chantones - What In The World's Come Over You

Disc: 4

1. Don Lang - Six-Five Special
2. Cliff Richard - Move It
3. Johnny Kidd & The Pirates - Shakin' All Over
4. Duane Eddy - Peter Gunn
5. Bobby Angelo & The Tuxedos - Baby Sittin'
6. Tony Crombie & The Rockets - Teach You To Rock
7. Tommy Bruce & The Bruisers - Ain't Misbehavin'
8. Shane Fenton & The Fentones - I'm A Moody Guy
9. Heinz - Just Like Eddie
10. Bobby Vee - Rubber Ball
11. The Chiffons - He's So Fine
12. Del Shannon - Hats Of To Larry
13. The Shadows - Foot Tapper
14. The Dakotas - The Cruel Sea
15. The Cougars - Saturday Nite At The Duck-Pond
16. Johnny Kidd & The Pirates - Please Don't Touch
17. Don Lang - Witch Doctor
18. Helen Shapiro - Don't Treat Me Like A Child
19. Adam Faith - What Do You Want
20. Craig Douglas - Only Sixteen
21. Cliff Richard - Please Don't Tease
22. Johnny Kidd & The Pirates - A Shot Of Rhythm & Blues

VARIOUS ARTISTS - ROCK 'N' ROLL: 72 CLASSICS FROM THE 50s & 60s (4CD)

Disc 1

All Shook Up - Elvis Presley
You Send Me - Sam Cooke
That'll Be The Day - The Crickets
Blue Suede Shoes - Carl Perkins
Good Golly Miss Molly - Little Richard
Summertime Blues - Eddie Cochrane
At The Hop - Danny & The Juniors
Too Much - Elvis Presley
Bony Maronie - Larry Williams
Tequilla - The Champs
Breathless - Jerry Lee Lewis
Endless Sleep - Marty Wilde
Rocking Pneumonia And Woogie Blues - Hucy Piano Smith
Along Came Jones - The Coasters
Heartbreak Hotel - Elvis Presley
Purple People Eaters - Sheb Wooley
Bongo Rock - Preston Epps
Mabellene - Chuck Berry

Disc 2

Jailhouse Rock - Elvis Presley
Oh Boy - Buddy Holly
Singing The Blues - Guy Mitchell
Rock N Roll Is Here To Stay - Danny & The Juniors
Teddy Bear - Elvis Presley
Sweet Little Rock And Roller - Chuck Berry
Diana - Paul Anka
A Teenage Romance - Ricky Nelson
Splish Splash - Bobby Darin
Don't Be Cruel - Elvis Presley
Teenage Crush - Tommy Sands
Rebel Rouser - Duan Eddy
A White Sport Coat (And A Pink Carnation) - Marty Robbins
Whole Lotta Woman - Marvin Rainwater
Sixteen Tons - Tennesse Ford
Hound Dog - Elvis Presley
Kansas City - Hank Ballard & The Midnighters
Johnny B. Goode - Chuck Berry

Disc 3

Rock Around The Clock - Bill Haley
Da Doo Ron Ron - The Crystals

Blueberry Hill - Fats Domino
Yakety Yak - The Coasters
Walk Right Back - Everly Brothers
Little Darlin' - The Diamonds
Red River Rock - Johnny & The Hurricanes
Lucille - Little Richard
Memphis Tennessee - Chuck Berry
Shake Rattle And Roll - Bill Haley
Claudette - Everly Brothers
One Fine Day - The Crystals
Tutti Fruitti - Little Richard
Jailhouse Rock - Carl Peters
Chantilly Lace - Tommy Bruce
Charlie Brown - The Coasters
Ain't That A Shame - Fats Domino
Sweet Little Sixteen - Chuck Berry
Disc 4
Great Balls Of Fire - Jerry Lee Lewis
Cathy's Clown - Everly Brothers
He's A Rebel - The Crystals
Long Tall Sally - Little Richard
Poison Ivy - The Coasters
My Blue Heaven - Fats Domino
Chapel Of Love - The Crystals
Reelin' And Rockin' - Chuck Berry
The Stroll - The Diamonds
Bye Bye Love - Everly Brothers
Whole Lotta Shakin' - Little Richard
Stagger Lee - Lloyd Price
Then He Kissed Me - The Crystals
Keep A Knockin' - Little Richard
Peppermint Twist - Joey & The Starlighters
Leader Of The Pack - Shangri-La's
Wake Up Little Suzie - Everly Brothers
Brown Eyed Handsome Man - Chuck Berry

VARIOUS-50S/ROCK & ROLL The Fabulous Fifties
(Original 1977 UK 159-track TEN vinyl LP box set.
No artists listed against songs.
Mule Train
I've Got A Lovely Bunch Of Coconuts
The Wedding Samba
I Remember The Cornfields
You're Breaking My Heart

100

The Old Piano Roll Blues
The French Can-Can Polka
Sentimental Me
Bewitched
Have I Told You Lately That I Love You?
If I Knew You Were Comin' I'dve Baked A Cake
Tennessee Waltz
Cherry Stones
Let's Do It Again
Dear Hearts and Gentle People
Christmas In Killarney
Ferry Boat Inn
On Top Of Old Smoky
Any Time
Too Young
Jezebel
The Petite Waltz
My Heart Cries For You
Because Of You
The Roving Kind
Shrimp Boats
Cold, Cold Heart
Mary Rose
Cone on-a My House
My Truly, Truly Fair
Rose, Rose, I Love You Unless
Some Enchanted Evening
There's ALways Room At Our House
We Won't Live In A Castle
Cry
High Noon (Do Not Foresake Me)
Blue Tango
The ISle Of Innisfree
Domino
Allentown Jail
The Homing Waltz At Teh End Of The Day
Down Yonder Be My Life's Comparison
Sugarbush
Be Anything (But Be Mine)
Kiss Of Fire
Outside Of Heaven
She Wears Red Feathers
(How Much Is) That Doggie In The Window?

Broken Wings
Oh, Happy Days
Somebody Stole My Gal
I Believe
In A Golden Coach (There's A Heart Of Gold)
Hold Me, Thrill Me, Kiss Me
The Song from Moulin Rouge (Where Is Your Heart?)
Hot Toddy
Let's Walk That- a-Way
Answer Me
Dragnet
Crying In The Chapel
I Saw Mommy Kissing Santa Claus
Blowing Wild
Cloud Lucky Seven
Let's Have Another Party Medley: Somebody Stole Me Gal / I Wonder
Where My Baby Is Tonight / When The Red Red Robin / Bye Bye
Blackbird / The Sheik Of Araby / Another Little Drink Medley: Lily Of
Laguna / Honeysuckle and the Bee / Broken Doll / Nellie Dean
I See The Moon
Skin Deep
Secret Love
Such A Night
The Kids
Last Fight
Friends and Neighbours
Cara Mia
The Little Shoemaker
This Ole House
Oh, Mein Papa Make
Love To Me
The Finger Of Suspicion
I Need You Now
Mambo Italiano
Tomorrow
Earth Angel
Ready, Willing and Able
I Wonder Everywhere
Stranger In Paradise
Cool Water
Blue Star
The Yellow Rose Of Texas
Hey There

The Man From Laramie
Hernanto's Hideaway
Twenty Tiny Fingers
Suddenly There's A Valley
The Ballad of Davy Crockett
Robin Hood
Band Of Gold
Memories Are Made Of This
My September Love
Lost John
The Theme from 'The Threepenny Opera'
Blue Suede Shoes
Whatever Will Be, Will Be
The Great Pretender
Lay Down Your Arms
Giddy-Up A Dong Dong
Woman In Love
The Green Door
Just Walkin' In The Rain
Rip It Up
The Garden Of Eden
Don't You Rock Me Daddy-O
The Adoration Waltz
Look Homeward Angel
The Banana Boat Song
Freight Train
Rock-a-Billy
We WIll Make Love
Little Darlin'
Gamblin Man'
Island In The Sun
Diana
With All My Heart I Love You Baby
Wake Up Little Susie
Great Balls Of Fire
Bony Moronie
You Are My Destiny
Story Of My Life
Love Me Forever
Nairobi Swingin'
Shepherd Blues
Grand Coulee Dam
A Certain Smile

Breathless
Twilight Time
On The Street Where You Live
Endless Sleep
Lillipop
Bird Dog
Tom Dooley
Hoots Man
As I Love You
High School Confidential
Petite Fleur
Smoke Gets In Your Eyes
Donna
My Little Drummer Boy
I've Waited So Long
The Battle Of New Orleans
The Heart Of A Man Someone Broken-Hearted Melody Till I Kissed You
Red River Rock Makin' Love Mr Blue Heartaches By The Number

VARIOUS-50s/R&B/ROCK & ROLL 20 Original Hits
(Scarce 60s US 20-track LP compilation, the vinyl
Jerry Butler - He Will Break Your Heart
Little Anthony & The Imperials - Tears On My Pillow
Ray Sharpe - Linda Lu
Marvin & Johnny - Cherry Pie
The Dubs - Could This Be Magic
The Innocents - Gee Whiz
Dee Clark - Just Keep It Up
Bobby Day - Little Bitty Pretty One
The Paris Sisters - I Love How You Love Me
Kathy Young - A Thousand Stars
Bobby Day - Rockin Robin
The Flamingos - I Only Have Eyes For You
The Penguins - Earth Angel
Eugene Church - Pretty Girls Everywhere
The Crystals - There's No Other
Jimmy Norman - Here Comes The Night
The Harptones - It All Depends On You
Rosie & The Originals - Angel Baby
The Youngsters - Dreamy Eyes
Jesse Belvin - Goodnight My Love

CLASSIC 60s
Disc 1:
Swinging Blue Jeans - Hippy Hippy Shake
Nashville Teens - Tobacco Road
The Animals - House Of The Rising Sun
Hollies - Carrie Anne
The Shadows - Kon-Tiki
Jeff Beck - Hi Ho Silver Lining
Manfred Man - Pretty Flamingo
Adam Faith - What Do You Want
Sandie Shaw - Long Live Love
Sounds Incorporated - William Tell
Herman's Hermits - No Milk Today
Peter & Gordon - Lady Godiva
Gerry & the Pacemakers - I Like It
Small Faces - Itchycoo Park
Petula Clark - You're The One
Disc 2:
The Marcels - Blue Moon
James Darren - Goodbye Cruel World
Joey Dee & Starlighters - Peppermint Twist
The Fifth Estate - Ding Dong The Witch Is Dead
Beach Boys - Good Vibrations
The Turtles - Happy Together
Canned Heat - On The Road Again
Sue Thompson - Paper Tiger
The Easybeats - She's So Fine
The Denvermen - Surfside
Russell Morris - The Real Thing
Billy Thorpe - Mashed Potatoes
Johnny Farnham - Sadie The Cleaning Lady
Brian Davies - Dream Girl
Johnny Ashcroft - Little Boy Lost
Disc 3:
Manfred Mann - Do Wah Diddy
The Shadows - Rise & Fall Of Flingal Bunt
The Animals - It's My Life
The Easybeats - Friday On My Mind
The Honeycombs - Have I The Right
Deep Purple - Kentucky Woman
Helen Shapiro - Not Responsible
The Hollies - Bus Stop
Peter & Gordon - A World Without Love

Gerry & The Pacemakers - Ferry Cross The Mersey
Billy J Kramer - Trains & Boats & Planes
Lulu - To Sir With Love
Frank Ifield - I Remember You
Rolf Harris - Tie me Kangaroo Down
The Seekers - I'll never Find Another You

THE GREATEST 60s HITS COLLECTION
CD 1
1. I'm Telling You Now - Freddie and The Dreamers
2. How Do You Do It? - Gerry and The Pacemakers
3. Tobacco Road - The Nashville Teens
4. The House of the Rising Sun - The Animals
5. I Get Around - The Beach Boys
6. Bus Stop - The Hollies
7. Shakin' All Over - Johnny Kidd & The Pirates
8. 5-4-3-2-1 - Manfred Mann
9. Mony Mony - Tommy James
10. I'm a Tiger - Lulu
11. F.B.I. - The Shadows
12. Georgy Girl - The Seekers
13. Aquarius - Paul Jones
14. Hurdy Gurdy Man - Donovan
15. A Message to Martha (Kentucky Bluebird) - Adam Faith
16. Rubber Ball - Bobby Vee
17. You're My World - Cilla Black
18. Got to Get You Into My Life - Cliff Bennett
19. Let's Have a Party - Wanda Jackson
20. Hi Ho Silver Lining - Jeff Beck
21. Three Steps to Heaven - Eddie Cochran
22. A Must to Avoid - Herman's Hermits
23. Sweet Talkin' City - The Chiffons
24. Happiness - Ken Dodd
25. Sun Arise - Rolf Harris
26. You're No Good - The Swinging Blue Jeans
27. Ob-la-di, Ob-la-da - Bedrocks
28. Love Letters in the Sand - Vince Hill
29. What Now My Love - Shirley Bassey
30. Galveston - Glen Campbell
Disc 2
1. Mellow Yellow - Donovan
2. Carrie Anne - The Hollies
3. Do You Want to Know a Secret? - Billy J. Kramer and The Dakotas
4. Walkin' Back to Happiness - Helen Shapiro

5. The Wanderer - Dion
6. I'm Into Something Good - Herman's Hermits
7. You Were Made for Me - Freddie and The Dreamers
8. Good Vibrations - The Beach Boys
9. Surf City - Jan and Dean
10. The Loco-motion - Little Eva
11. Dreamin' - Johnny Burnette
12. Tell Laura I Love Her - Ricky Valance
13. Blue Moon - The Marcels
14. More Than I Can Say - Bobby Vee
15. True Love Ways - Peter Gordon
16. I Remember You - Frank Ifield
17. Pretty Flamingo - Manfred Mann
18. The Boat That I Row - Lulu
19. We've Gotta Get Out of This Place - The Animals
20. I'm a Moody Guy - Shane Fenton and The Fentones
21. With a Little Help from My Friends - The Young Idea
22. I'm the Urban Spaceman - The Bonzo Dog Doo Dah Band
23. Spooky - Classics IV
24. You'll Never Walk Alone - Gerry and The Pacemakers
25. You've Lost That Loving Feeling - Cilla Black
26. Hold Me - P.J. Proby
27. Stingray - The Shadows
28. Walk Don't Run - The Ventures
29. Cruel Sea - The Dakotas
30. 'James Bond' Theme - The John Barry Seven

PURE CROONERS
CD 1
1. Andy Williams - Love Story (Where Do I Begin)
2. Tony Bennett - A Taste Of Honey
3. Perry Como - Magic Moments
4. Bing Crosby - Mamma Loves Papa
5. Paul Anka - Put Your Head On My Shoulder
6. Johnnie Ray - Cry
7. Eddie Fisher - Downhearted
8. Frank Sinatra - All Or Nothing At All
9. Mel Tormé - P.S. I Love You
10. Vic Damone - Gigi
11. John Gary - Time After Time
12. Jerry Vale - Volare (Nel blu, dipinto di blu)
13. Billy Paul - Me And Mrs. Jones
14. Ray Price - For The Good Times
15. Charlie Rich - The Most Beautiful Girl

107

16. The Union Gap feat. Gary Puckett - Young Girl
17. Elvis Presley - The Wonder Of You
CD 2
1. Jim Reeves - He'll Have To Go
2. Harry Belafonte - Try To Remember
3. Frank Sinatra - The Girl That I Marry
4. Anthony Newley - What Kind Of Fool Am I?
5. Eddy Arnold - Make The World Go Away
6. Louis Armstrong And His All-Stars - Mack The Knife
7. Jerry Vale - Promises, Promises
8. Bobby Vinton - Blue On Blue
9. Neil Sedaka - Oh Carol
10. Frankie Laine - I Believe
11. Tony Martin - Stranger In Paradise
12. The Browns - The Three Bells
13. Mac Davis - Baby, Don't Get Hooked On Me
14. Johnny Nash - Cupid
15. Georgie Fame - Because I Love You
16. Engelbert Humperdinck - Release Me (Live)
17. Julio Iglesias - Begin The Beguine (Volver a empezar)
CD 3
1. Elvis Presley - Love Me Tender
2. Johnny Mathis - Chances Are
3. Bing Crosby - Dream A Little Dream Of Me
4. Mel Tormé - I've Got You Under My Skin
5. Tony Bennett - I Left My Heart In San Francisco
6. Andy Williams - Speak Softly Love
7. Perry Como - (They Long To Be) Close To You
8. Bobby Vinton - Roses Are Red (My Love)
9. Harry Belafonte - Day-O (The Banana Boat Song)
10. Marty Robbins - Devil Woman
11. Guy Mitchell - She Wears Red Feathers
12. Paul Anka - You Are My Destiny
13. Mario Lanza - Because You're Mine
14. Vic Damone - An Affair To Remember
15. José Feliciano - And The Sun Will Shine
16. Brook Benton - A Nightingale Sang In Berkeley Square
17. Harold Melvin - If You Don't Know Me By Now
CD 4
1. Barry Manilow - Mandy
2. Michael Bolton - How Am I Supposed To Live Without You
3. Curtis Stigers - I Wonder Why
4. Johnny Logan - Hold Me Now

5. Shakin' Stevens - Because I Love You
6. Julio Iglesias & Willie Nelson - To All The Girls I've Loved Before
7. Engelbert Humperdinck - Perfect Love
8. Luther Vandross - Here And Now
9. Marvin Gaye - Sexual Healing
10. Johnny Mathis - I'm Stone In Love With You
11. Roger Whittaker - The Last Farewell
12. The Walker Brothers - No Regrets
13. Michael Ball - Fever
14. Buster Poindexter - Hit The Road Jack
15. Steve Tyrell - It Had To Be You
16. Rick Astley - When I Fall In Love
17. Il Divo - The Power Of Love (La fuerza mayor

PURE 60s
Disc 1
We've Gotta Get Out Of This Place - The Animals
Mony Mony - Tommy James And The Shondells
Sha La La - Manfred Mann
I Get Around - The Beach Boys
Just One Look - The Hollies
F.B.I. - The Shadows
I'm A Tiger - Lulu
You Were Made For Me - Freddie & The Dreamers
Runaway - Del Shannon
Walkin' Back To Happiness - Helen Shapiro
I Like It - Gerry & The Pacemakers
Sunshine Girl - Herman's Hermits
Bad To Me - Billy J Kramer & The Dakotas
Tobacco Road - The Nashville
Poison Ivy - The Paramounts
Jenny Takes A Ride - Mitch Ryder & The Detroit Wheels
On The Road Again - Canned Heat
Living In The Past - Jethro Tull
I'm The Urban Spaceman - The Bonzo Dog Doo Dah Band
Kites - Simon Dupree & The Big Sound
Up Up And Away - The Johnny Mann Singers
Spooky - Classics IV
The Cruel Sea - The Dakotas
The Magnificent Seven - John Barry
African Waltz - Johnny Dankworth
Disc 2
Leader Of The Pack - Shangri-La's
He's So Fine - The Chiffons

109

Tell Him - Exciters
The Wanderer - Dion
Hey! Baby - Bruce Channel
You're Sixteen - Johnny Burnette
Travelin' Man - Ricky Nelson
Good Golly Miss Molly - The Swinging Blue Jeans
Shakin' All Over - Johnny Kidd & The Pirates
(They Call Her) La Bamba - The Crickets
Apache - Bert Weedon
Pistol Packin' Mama - Gene Vincent
The Locomotion - Little Eva
Let's Have A Party - Wanda Jackson
Peppermint Twist - Joey Dee & The Starlighters
Walking To New Orleans - Fats Domino
Perfidia - The Ventures
It's All Over Now - Shane Fenton & The Fentones
Ain't Misbehavin' - Tommy Bruce & The Bruisers
Drink Up Thy Zider - Adge Cutler & The Wurzels
Seven Drunken Nights - The Dubliners
Thank U Very Much - The Scaffold
Ob-La-Di Ob-La-Da - Bedrocks
Tie Me Kangaroo Down Sport - Rolf Harris 2.40
Right Said Fred - Bernard Cribbins
Disc 3
Poor Me - Adam Faith
Poetry In Motion - Johnny Tillotson 2.30
Take Good Care Of My Baby (1961 Version) - Bobby Vee
Where Do You Go To (My Lovely) - Peter Sarstedt
True Love Ways - Peter And Gordon
Morningtown Ride - The Seekers
You've Lost That Lovin' Feelin' - Cilla Black
Hello Little Girl - The Fourmost
One Way Love - Cliff Bennett & The Rebel Rousers
Hold Me - P J Proby
Mockingbird - Inez Foxx And Charlie Foxx
When My Little Girl Is Smiling - Craig Douglas
She Wears My Ring - Solomon King
From Russia With Love - Matt Monro
Promises - Ken Dodd
I Pretend - Des O'Connor
Up On The Roof - Kenny Lynch
Lovesick Blues - Frank Ifield
A Windmill In Old Amsterdam - Ronnie Hilton

Starry Eyed - Michael Holliday
Moon River - Danny Williams
Galveston - Glen Campbell
Games People Play - Joe South
Ode To Billie Joe - Bobbie Gentry
The Weight - The Band

ALL THE 60s
Disc 1:
The Shirelles - Will You Love Me Tomorrow?
Gene Pitney - The Man Who Shot Liberty Valance
Del Shannon - Runaway
The Archies - Sugar Sugar
Eddie Hodges - I'm Gonna Knock On Your Door
The Monkees - I'm A Believer
The Everly Brothers - Cathy's Clown
Bobby Darin - Dream Lover
Trini Lopez - If I Had A Hammer
Edison Lighthouse - Love Grows (Where Rosemary Goes)
Paul & Paula - Hey Paula
Frankie Valli - Can't Take My Eyes Off You
Esther Phillips - And I Love Him
The Association - Cherish
Ned Miller - From A Jack To A King
Mel Torme - Cast Your Fate To The Winds
Disc 2:
Aretha Franklin - I Say A Little Prayer
The Drifters - Save The Last Dance For Me
Otis Redding - (Sittin' On) The Dock Of The Bay
Frankie Valli & The Four Seasons - Big Girls Don't Cry
Sonny & Cher -I Got You Babe
Percy Sledge - When A Man Loves A Woman
Sam & Dave - Hold On, I'm Coming
Ray Charles - I Got A Woman
Jackie Wilson - (Your Love Keeps Lifting Me) Higher
Eddie Floyd - Knock On Wood
Clarence Carter - Slip Away
Dionne Warwick - I Just Don't Know What To Do With Myself
Wilson Pickett - Land Of 1000 Dances
Booker T. & The MG's - Green Onions
Ben E. King - Spanish Harlem
Arthur Conley - Sweet Soul Music

Disc 3:

Normie Rowe - Shakin' All Over
Johnny O'Keefe - She's My Baby
Tony Joe White - Polk Salad Annie
Buffalo Springfield - For What It's Worth
R.B. Greaves - Take A Letter, Maria
Ray Brown - The Same Old Song
Eddie Harris - I'm Gonna Leave You By Yourself
Cascades - Rhythm Of The Rain
The Fireballs - Bottle of Wine
Vanilla Fudge - You Keep Me Hangin' On
Jack Nitzsche - The Lonely Surfer
Johnny & The Hurricanes - Beatnik Fly
B.J. Thomas - Mama
Solomon Burke - Everybody Needs Somebody To Love
Billy Pilgrim - Mama Says
Lonnie Mack - I Found A Love

DANIEL O'DONNELL - THE ROCK 'N' ROLL SHOW (DVD)

Come On Over To My Place
Oh Boy
When You Walk In The Room
Three Steps To Heaven
Twelfth Of Never
That'll Be The Day
Poetry In Motion
My Boy Lollipop (Mary Duff)
You Never Can Tell (Mary Duff)
Walk Right Back (Duet)
Calendar Girl
Elvis Medley: Blue Suede Shoes / Good Luck Charm / Love Me Tender /
All Shook Up
Words
Teenager In Love
Lipstick On Your Collar
Johnny B. Goode (Mary Duff)
Beautiful Sunday
Wonderful Tonight
You're Sixteen
Girl Of My best Friend
Hopelessly Devoted To You (Mary Duff)
Beatles Medley: All My Loving / Hey Jude / Yesterday / Ticket To Ride
Is This The Way to Amarillo

The Moon Of Love Medley: Dream Lover / Single Girl / I'm A Believer /
Bobby's Girl/ When / Don't Go Breaking My Heart / It's In His Kiss / Da
Do Ron Ron / And Then I Kissed Her / Under The Moon Of Love
Jailhouse Rock (Billy)
Only Sixteen
Be My Guest
Ole Man Trouble
Knock Three Times
Where The Boys Are (Mary Duff)
The Carnival Is Over (Duet)
But I Do
Daydream Believer
Donna
At The Hop (John)
Cliff Richard Medley: Living Doll / Young Ones / Summer Holiday/
Miss You Nights/
Do You Want To Dance
Walking Back To Happiness
Ob-la-di,Ob-la-da
Living Next Door To Alice
Rockin' Robin (Mary Duff)
Let's Twist Again
Let's Dance
Encore - Rock Around The Clock

VARIOUS ARTISTS ROCK 'N' ROLL JUKEBOX: HITS
FROM THE '50s & '60s
Disc 1
1 -The Great Pretender -The Platters
2 -Little Darlin' -The Diamonds
3 -Come Go with Me -The Del Vikings
4 -Rave On -Buddy Holly
5 -I'm Sorry -Brenda Lee
6 -Sh-Boom -The Crew Cuts
7 -See You Later Alligator Bill Haley & His Comets
8 -Sweet Little Sixteen -Chuck Berry
9 -Who Do You Love? -Bo Diddley
10 -Stagger Lee -Lloyd Price
11 -Rescue Me -Fontella Bass
12 -You've Lost That Lovin' Feeling -Phil Spector The Righteous
Brothers
Disc 2
1 -Stand By Me -Ben E. King / Jerry Leiber / Mike Stoller -Ben E. King
2 -Bye Bye Love -The Everly Brothers

3 -Why Do Fools Fall in Love -Frankie Lymon & the Teenagers
4 -La Bamba –Traditional -Ritchie Valens
5 -Mack the Knife -Kurt Weill -Bobby Darin
6 -Mr. Lee -Ben E. King -The Bobbettes
7 -What'd I Say, Pts. 1-2 Ray Charles
8 -Mustang Sally -Wilson Pickett
9 -Just One Look -Doris Troy
10 -Searchin' -Jerry Leiber / Mike Stoller - The Coasters
11 -Green Onions -Steve Cropper / Al Jackson, Jr. / Lewis Steinberg -
Booker T. & the MG's
12 -Save the Last Dance for Me -Doc Pomus / Mort Shuman -The
Drifters

Disc 3

1 -Summertime Blues -Jerry Capehart / Eddie Cochran - Eddie Cochran
2 -Runaround Sue -Dion DiMucci - Dion
3 -Surf City -Chuck Berry - Jan & Dean
4 –Tequila -The Champs
5 -Be-Bop-a-Lula -Gene Vincent & the Blue Caps
6 -Blue Monday -Dave Bartholomew
7 –Mockingbird --Inez & Charlie Foxx
8 -Mr. Blue -The Fleetwoods
9 -Be True to Your School -The Beach Boys
10 -26 Miles (Santa Catalina)-The Four Preps
11 -Stood Up -Rick Nelson

50's & 60's ROCK 'N ROLL

At The Hop...Danny & The Juniors
Ain't Too Proud To Beg...Temptations
All Shook Up...Elvis
Birthday...Beatles
Blue Suede Shoes...Elvis
Brown Eyed Girl...Van Morrison
California Girls...Beach Boys
Can't Help Falling In Love...Elvis
Chantilly Lace...The Big Bopper
Chapel of Love...Dixie Cups
Dance To The Music...Sly Stone
Devil With The Blue Dress On...Mitch Ryder
Doo Wah Diddy...Manfred Mann
Do You Love Me...Contours
Fun, Fun, Fun...Beach Boys
Gloria...Them
Great Balls Of Fire...Jerry Lee Lewis
Heatwave...Martha Reeves / Vandellas

Hound Dog...Elvis
I Can't Help Myself...Four Tops
I Feel Good...James Brown
I Get Around...Beach Boys
I Heard It Though The Grapevine...Marvin Gaye
Iki Iko...Belle Stars
In The Still Of The Night...The Five Satins
Jailhouse Rock...Elvis
Kansas City...Wilbert Harrison
La Bamba...Richie Valens / Los Lobos
Little Deuce Coupe...Beach Boys
Louie Louie...Kingsmen
Love Me Tender...Elvis
Mack The Knife...Bobby Darin
Maybelline...Chuck Berry
Mony Mony...Tommy James
My Girl...Temptations
Pretty Woman...Roy Orbison
Proud Mary...Creedence Clearwater
Respect...Aretha Franklin
Rock Around The Clock...Bill Haley
Rock & Roll Music...Beatles
Roll Over Beethoven...Beatles
Runaround Sue...Dion
Runaway...Del Shannon
Satisfaction...Stones
Shout...Isley Brothers
Shotgun...Jr. Walker
Sittin' On The Dock Of The Bay...Otis Redding
Soul Man...Sam & Dave
Stand By Me...Ben E. King
Surfin' USA...Beach Boys
Tequila...Champs
The Hokey Pokey...Ray Anthony
The Stroll...The Diamonds
The Twist...Chubby Checker
Tutti Frutti...Little Richard
Twist & Shout...Beatles
Unchained Melody...Righteous Brothers
What A Wonderful World...Louis Armstrong
What'd I Say...Ray Charles
When A Man Loves A Woman...Percy Sledge
Willie And The Hand Jive...Johnny Otis

Whole Lotta Shakin' Goin On...Jerry Lee Lewis
Wipeout...Safaris
Wooly Bully...Sam The Sham & The Pharaohs
You Never Can Tell (Pulp Fiction)...Chuck Berry
You've Lost That Lovin' Feeling...Righteous Brothers

100 GREATEST ROCK 'N' ROLL SONGS OF THE '50s
1. Johnny B. Goode - Chuck Berry
2. Jailhouse Rock - Elvis Presley
3. Rock Around The Clock - Bill Haley & His Comets
4. Tutti-Frutti - Little Richard
5. Whole Lot of Shakin' Going On - Jerry Lee Lewis
6. What'd I Say - Ray Charles
7. Summertime Blues - Eddie Cochran
8. Hound Dog - Elvis Presley
9. Long Tall Sally - Little Richard
10. That'll Be The Day - Buddy Holly & the Crickets
11. Maybellene - Chuck Berry
12. Bo Diddley - Bo Diddley
13. Shake, Rattle And Roll - Joe Turner
14. Blue Suede Shoes - Carl Perkins
15. Don't Be Cruel - Elvis Presley
16. Bye Bye Love - Everly Brothers
17. Great Balls Of Fire - Jerry Lee Lewis
18. Earth Angel - Penguins
19. Why Do Fools Fall In Love - Frankie Lymon & the Teenagers
20. Good Golly Miss Molly - Little Richard
21. Be-Bop-A-Lula - Gene Vincent & the Bluecaps
22. School Day - Chuck Berry
23. Rock And Roll Music - Chuck Berry
24. Peggy Sue - Buddy Holly
25. Lawdy Miss Clawdy - Lloyd Price
26. Lucille - Little Richard
27. Roll Over Beethoven - Chuck Berry
28. In The Still Of The Nite - Five Satins
29. I Only Have Eyes For You – Flamingos
30. For Your Precious Love - Jerry Butler & the Impressions
31. Blueberry Hill - Fats Domino
32. Please, Please, Please - James Brown & the Famous Flames
33. Sh-Boom - Chords
34. Money Honey - Drifters featuring Clyde McPhatter
35. I Walk The Line - Johnny Cash and the Tennessee Two
36. Heartbreak Hotel - Elvis Presley
37. Fever - Little Willie John

116

38. The Great Pretender - Platters
39. Ain't It A Shame - Fats Domino
40. That's All Right - Elvis Presley with Scotty and Bill
41. Your Cheatin' Heart - Hank Williams
42. Sweet Little Sixteen - Chuck Berry
43. The Train Kept-A-Rollin - Johnny Burnette Trio
44. Come Go With Me - Del-Vikings
45. Let The Good Times Roll - Shirley & Lee
46. Rip It Up - Little Richard
47. Rocking Pneumonia & the Boogie Woogie Flu - Huey "Piano" Smith
& the Clowns
48. Pledging My Love - Johnny Ace
49. Sixty Minute Man - Dominoes
50. Rocket 88 - Jackie Brenston
51. Yakety Yak - Coasters
52. All Shook Up - Elvis Presley
53. Folsom Prison Blues - Johnny Cash and the Tennessee Two
54. Searchin' - Coasters
55. You Send Me - Sam Cooke
56. Mack The Knife - Bobby Darin
57. Wake Up Little Susie - Everly Brothers
58. Susie Q - Dale Hawkins
59. La Bamba - Ritchie Valens
60. Goodnite, Sweetheart, Goodnite - Spaniels
61. I've Got A Woman - Ray Charles
62. I'm Walkin' - Fats Domino
63. There Goes My Baby - Drifters
64. Shout - Isley Brothers
65. White Christmas - Drifters featuring Clyde McPhatter
66. Keep A 'Knockin' - Little Richard
67. Kansas City - Wilbert Harrison
68. Poison Ivy - Coasters
69. Since I Don't Have You - Skyliners
70. Jambalaya (On The Bayou) - Hank Williams
71. Money - Barrett Strong
72. Speedoo - Cadillacs
73. Rumble - Link Wray
74. Lonely Teardrops - Jackie Wilson
75. Hang Up My Rock And Roll Shoes - Chuck Willis
76. Sea Cruise - Frankie Ford
77. Rave On - Buddy Holly
78. Work With Me Annie - Hank Ballard & the Midnighters
79. Shake, Rattle And Roll - Bill Haley & His Comets

80. Sincerely - Moonglows
81. Crying In The Chapel - Sonny Til & the Orioles
82. Story Untold - Nutmegs
83. My Babe - Little Walter
84. At My Front Door - El Dorados
85. Gee - Crows
86. Matchbox - Carl Perkins
87. C.C. Rider - Chuck Willis
88. Only You - Platters
89. All I Have To Do Is Dream - Everly Brothers
90. Send Me Some Lovin' - Little Richard
91. At The Hop - Danny & the Juniors
92. Little Darlin' - Diamonds
93. Rock-in Robin - Bobby Day
94. Honky Tonk - Bill Doggett
95. Blue Monday - Fats Domino
96. Jim Dandy - Lavern Baker
97. Reelin And Rocking - Chuck Berry
98. Rebel Rouser - Duane Eddy
99. Love Potion No. 9 - Clovers
100. Chantilly Lace - Big Bopper
101. Oh Boy! - Buddy Holly & the Crickets
102. Get A Job - Silhouettes
103. Book Of Love - Monotones
104. C'mon Everybody - Eddie Cochran
105. Do You Want To Dance - Bobby Freeman
106. Willie And The Hand Jive - Johnny Otis Show
107. You're So Fine - Falcons
108. Handy Man - Jimmy Jones
109. Sea Of Love - Phil Phillips with the Twilights
110. Breathless - Jerry Lee Lewis
111. Stagger Lee - Lloyd Price
112. Tequila - Champs
113. It's Only Make Believe - Conway Twitty
114. Have Mercy Baby - Dominoes
115. Maybe Baby - Buddy Holly & the Crickets
116. Young Blood - Coasters
117. Little Bitty Pretty One - Thurston Harris
118. Not Fade Away - Buddy Holly & the Crickets
119. The Fat Man - Fats Domino
120. Baby Let's Play House - Elvis Presley with Scotty and Bill
121. Mystery Train - Elvis Presley with Scotty and Bill
122. Tweedlee Dee - LaVern Baker

123. One Mint Julep - Clovers
124. Shake A Hand - Faye Adams
125. Honey Hush - Joe Turner
126. Tears On My Pillow - Little Anthony & the Imperials
127. Oh What A Nite - Dells
128. My Prayer - Platters
129. Dizzy Miss Lizzy - Larry Williams
130. Who Do You Love - Bo Diddley
131. Brown-Eyed Handsome Man - Chuck Berry
132. Ready Teddy - Little Richard
133. Honey Don't - Carl Perkins
134. I'm In Love Again - Fats Domino
135. Little Girl Of Mine - Cleftones
136. A Thousand Miles Away - Heartbeats
137. Tear It Up - Johnny Burnette Trio
138. Blue Suede Shoes - Elvis Presley
139. Drown In My Own Tears - Ray Charles
140. I Put A Spell On You - Screamin' Jay Hawkins
141. Love Is Strange - Mickey & Sylvia
142. I'm A Man - Bo Diddley
143. Unchained Melody - Al Hibbler
144. See You Later, Alligator - Bill Haley & His Comets
145. Around And Around - Chuck Berry
146. Don't You Just Know It - Huey "Piano" Smith & the Clowns
147. One Night - Elvis Presley
148. Carol - Chuck Berry
149. What Am I Living For - Chuck Willis
150. Sixteen Candles - Crests
151. Smoke Gets In Your Eyes - Platters
152. Bird Dog - Everly Brothers
153. Baby What You Want Me To Do - Jimmy Reed
154. A Teenager In Love - Dion & the Belmonts
155. Splish Splash - Bobby Darin
156. I'm Ready - Fats Domino
157. I Wonder Why - Dion & the Belmonts
158. Charlie Brown - Coasters
159. Rock And Roll Is Here To Stay - Danny & the Juniors
160. Back In The U.S.A. - Chuck Berry
161. Come Softly To Me - Fleetwoods
162. Beyond The Sea - Bobby Darin
163. Night Train - Jimmy Forrest
164. When You Dance - Turbans
165. The Wallflower - Etta James

166. Whole Lotta Loving - Fats Domino
167. Flip, Flop And Fly - Joe Turner
168. (Night Time Is) The Right Time - Ray Charles
169. Mama, He Treats Your Daughter Mean - Ruth Brown
170. Good Rocking Tonight - Elvis Presley with Scotty and Bill
171. Come On Let's Go - Ritchie Valens
172. Walking After Midnight - Patsy Cline
173. I'm A King Bee - Slim Harpo
174. Got My Mojo Working - Muddy Waters
175. Goodnight My Love - Jessie Belvin
176. Day-O (Banana Boat Song) - Harry Belafonte
177. Stranded In The Jungle - Cadets
178. I Just Want To Make Love To You - Muddy Waters
179. Hearts Of Stone - Charms
180. Jingle Bell Rock - Bobby Helms
181. Too Much - Elvis Presley
182. Diana - Paul Anka
183. Dedicated To The One I Love - Shirelles
184. Silhouettes - Rays
185. Honey Love - Drifters featuring Clyde McPhatter
186. Lovey Dovey - Clovers
187. Hoochie Coochie Man - Muddy Waters
188. Dust My Broom - Elmore James
189. Dream Lover - Bobby Darin
190. It's Late - Ricky Nelson
191. Sleep Walk - Santo & Johnny
192. Reet Petite - Jackie Wilson
193. Don't Let Go - Roy Hamilton
194. Sweet Nothin's - Brenda Lee
195. Fannie Mae - Buster Brown
196. Hey Little Girl - Dee Clark
197. Short Fat Fannie - Larry Williams
198. The Wind - Diablos
199. Rock Island Line - Lonnie Donegan
200. Harlem Nocturne – Viscounts

BIBLIOGRAPHY

https://itunes.apple.com/us/album/best-rock-n-roll-greatest/id739730835
BEST OF ROCK 'N' ROLL - GREATEST ORIGINALS FROM THE
50S & 60S
100 GREATEST HITS OF ROCK 'N' ROLL VARIOUS ARTISTS
http://www.discogs.com/Various-Rock-N-Roll-Hits-50s-
60s/release/3767817
VARIOUS– ROCK N' ROLL HITS 50s & 60s 3 × CD, COMPILATION
http://www.discogs.com/Various-Baby-Love-100-Classic-Love-Songs-
Of-The-50s-And-60s/release/1678254
VARIOUS– BABY LOVE - 100 CLASSIC LOVE SONGS OF THE 50's
And 60's 4 × CD, COMPILATION BOX SET
http://www.amazon.co.uk/101-Rock-N-Roll-
Hits/dp/tracks/B0018CWWEG/ref=dp_tracks_all_4/280-5781096-
4494748#disc_4
101 ROCK N ROLL HITS [BOX SET]
http://www.walmart.ca/en/ip/various-artists-rock-n-roll-72-classics-from-
the-50s-60s-4cd/6000038639988
VARIOUS ARTISTS - ROCK 'N' ROLL: 72 CLASSICS FROM THE
50s & 60s (4CD)
http://eil.com/shop/wanted.asp?artist=Various--50s/Rock-_-
Roll/Rockabilly
VARIOUS-50S/ROCK & ROLL The Fabulous Fifties (Original 1977 UK
159-track TEN vinyl LP box set. No artists listed against songs.
VARIOUS-50s/R&B/ROCK & ROLL 20 Original Hits (Scarce 60s US
20-track LP compilation, the vinyl
http://www.jukeboxhits.com.au/Classic%2060s%20Track%20List.
CLASSIC 60s; THE GREATEST 60s HITS COLLECTION
PURE CROONERS; PURE 60s; All THE 60s
http://www.ovationchannel.com.au/catalog/product/view/id/4585/s/daniel
-odonnell-the-rock-n-roll-show/category/15/
DANIEL O'DONNELL - THE ROCK 'N' ROLL SHOW (DVD)
http://www.allmusic.com/album/rock-n-roll-jukebox-hits-from-the-50s-
60s-mw0002362035
VARIOUS ARTISTS ROCK 'N' ROLL JUKEBOX: HITS FROM THE
'50s & '60s
http://www.musicnowdj.com/index/50's+%26+60's+Rock+'n+Roll
50's & 60's ROCK 'N ROLL
http://digitaldreamdoor.com/pages/best_songs50s.html
100 GREATEST ROCK 'N' ROLL SONGS OF THE '50s

ABOUT THE AUTHOR

I was 59 years old; a mother of three very special and supportive adult children and a grandmother of three wonderful grandsons (I now have five grand-children.) when I started writing my first book whilst watching a Bon Jovi concert DVD. (I am an avid fan, if you can call me that; crazy is more like it.)

I write from the heart and I really enjoyed writing the book so I wrote another using a different artist, and the books kept coming to me and I kept writing them.(with a little help from above)

Because I use different artist/artists song titles I have to be very careful with Copyright so a lot of legal requirements have to be taken into consideration before publishing the books. I also needed a name that would connect my books to each other; so the "Song Title Series" books began.

All my books are short stories; however it depends on how many song titles there are to be used, as to the length of the book. Some artists didn't have enough song titles on their own so I combined them with a few other artists. Other artists had that many song titles that I could have written a novel; but it would have ended up being boring.

Challenges I like, so writing books with various artists are a lot of fun and require careful thinking.

Why should I have all the fun writing the books and not be able to share them with everyone; so I have converted them into large print books so that you can share my fun as well.

Hopefully in the not too distant future; the books will also be available as audio books so that no-one will miss out on my fun and enjoyment of writing these unique books. I hope that you enjoy reading them.

My web site www.songtitleseries.com is the place to visit for updates of new books and a place to purchase other titles in other formats.

TESTIMONIALS

Joan Maguire Books are very nice, I enjoy reading them so much, they are hard to put down!! Especially when she does one about Bonjovi and their songs!!!
If I can say, it is worth every penny, when you buy one!!! The Books make nice presents, for a person whom loves to read!!! I can guarantee that you will LOVE these books, because I do!!!!!!!!!
Dawn from Newark, Delaware in the United States of America

I am Susie and would like to tell you guys, how much I am enjoying Joan Maguire's Books!! They are very enjoyable, and they are something that you do not ever want to put down!! I really enjoy these books; I can't wait until the next one that she puts out!!!!!!! I say go to your local book store, today and get one, you will not be disappointed!!!!!
Sue-from the United States of America

After reading through your range of books I felt I must compliment you Joan on the imaginative and entertaining way in which you presented each group and the Musicians in those groups. The way the stories were constructed is a credit to your work ethic. These must have taken considerable time to piece together and it is obviously a work of love for you.
I wish you all the success you truly deserve and look forward to seeing you next time you visit Tamworth.
Peter Harkins
Managing Director Cheapa Music
Country Music Capital Tamworth

The song titles series are books that were intriguing and were hard to believe that these short stories were written within the incorporated song titles of the artists that are mentioned in the titles. I loved what I have read so far and think that anyone with an imagination and love of music as the author you will surely enjoy reading these.
L.K. Brisbane Australia.

www.ingramcontent.com/pod-product-compliance
Lightning Source LLC
Chambersburg PA
CBHW072004170626
46813CB00005B/2011